Twisting her head
to see how far she was i
have to jump.

Suddenly, both shoes slid away, her tenuous hold gone. Cursing as her hands parted company with the rough bark, she fell heavily on top of a solid mound.

The mound moved.

And groaned.

Before she had time to react she was forcefully ejected and pitched onto her side. A heavy weight then knocked her flat on her back, one large hand covering her mouth.

"What the devil...?" The deep voice rumbled in her ears. The man looming over her appeared to be wearing a uniform. Pine needles were stuck to his collar. His face was close enough for her to feel his breath and the dark pools of his eyes glared into hers.

Stealthily, Louisa's hand crept towards her pocket.

He gave a grunt of astonishment. "A woman?"

She made to whip out a revolver, but he was too quick for her. He clamped a hand on each of her wrists. She was no match for his strength.

"What are you doing here?" he demanded. His grip tightened when she didn't answer. "Who are you?"

French Kiss

by

Cherie Le Clare

To Roger!
With appreciation
for your support
and best wishes,
from your cousin,
Cherie Le Clare.
May, 2010.

French Kiss

Cover Art by *Nicola Martinez*

The Wild Rose Press
PO Box 708
Adams Basin, NY 14410-0706
Visit us at www.thewildrosepress.com

Publishing History
First Vintage Rose Edition, 2010

Published in the United States of America

Dedication

I dedicate this book to my husband, family, friends
and my editor. Without their generous
encouragement, I would not have
made it this far.

Prologue
Paris, France 1939

"They've got Harry!" Louisa, panting heavily, burst into the typing room.

Monique, engrossed in examining her manicure, barely glanced up. She inquired, in a bored tone, "Ze Nazis?"

"Yes!" Louisa itched to shake the Frenchwoman out of her apathy. "The Nazis!" She gulped in a ragged breath and glanced into the boss's office. "Where's M'sieur...?"

"Papa can't help," Monique dismissed flatly. "He's at a meeting." She added with a shrug, "And no one else iz here."

Louisa, her heart sinking, turned to the window and glanced down. Harry was being pushed and shoved between three thugs. One of them dragged the canvas bag off Harry's arm and drew out a handful of leaflets. With a whoop of hysteria, he ripped them to shreds and threw them into the air. The swastika on his arm band was clearly visible.

"*Merde!*"

At Louisa's curse, Monique sauntered over and tapped one scarlet-painted, sharp fingernail against the glass. "Tell me, s'il vous plait, what is printed on ze leaflets?"

"See for yourself." Louisa snatched one out of her bag and handed it over.

As she read, Monique's eyes narrowed. "Foolish man," she muttered. "I warned him not to write—"

"Warned?" Louisa interrupted, astonished.

Monique, avoiding her gaze, merely drew her lips into a thin line of disapproval.

This strange response barely registered with Louisa as she caught a glimpse of Harry's face. Her blood ran cold.

"Phone the gendarmerie!" she hurled at Monique before running back down the stairs.

A small crowd had gathered. A grey-bearded man stepped forward, bravely commanding the youths to stop. Louisa watched, wide-eyed with horror as, along with flinging insults, the larger one of the attackers punched the man in the stomach, forcing him to his knees.

Harry was thrown back against the outside wall of the building. Louisa winced. She glanced both ways down the street. Where were the gendarmes? *Police.* Why were they so slow? Harry groaned as a heavy boot connected with his shin.

"Leave him alone!" Louisa yelled at the perpetrator, her heart pumping fast. She lunged, furiously beating with both fists against the lout's back. He swung round and, with one hefty swipe against her shoulder, knocked her, staggering, into the loose circle of bystanders. Advancing menacingly, he glared at her. The evil glint in his pale blue eyes made the hairs stand up on the back of her neck.

She turned and fled, her shoes clacking loudly up the stairs. Slamming the door shut, she locked it behind her. Breathing heavily, she paused to listen for any sounds of pursuit. But there were none. Cautiously, she crept to the window and closed the blinds, leaving only a slit to see through.

Where were the gendarmes? Louisa glanced around for Monique but the office was deserted. With a horrid sense of foreboding, she forced herself to peer below. She gasped, her hand over her mouth, sickened by each vicious punch. Harry's desperate cries sliced through her like a knife. She ran to phone the gendarmerie again, her fingers clumsy, her speech halting, and she groaned in disbelief when she was told that hers was the first call for help they'd received.

The first? Why hadn't Monique phoned them?

"Hurry!" she pleaded. She raced back to the window. Two of the brutes had dragged him across the street and were slipping into a dark, narrow alley.

Louisa never saw Harry again.

Chapter One
Normandy, France 1944

Louisa stared down into the dark, empty void. All lights were hidden behind blackout curtains. She forced herself to concentrate on what she'd been taught in training on how to land safely. She checked, for the final time, the adjustment of her parachute straps.

"Dropping zone ahead," the pilot's voice crackled through the intercom. Louisa glanced at her fellow agent. He gave her the thumbs-up sign.

As the French countryside, six hundred feet below, revealed itself under a soft moonlight, the wind whipped the legs of her overalls. She patted each of her deep coat pockets, reassuring herself that her revolvers were secure.

Rolling her shoulders to ease the weight of the kitbag, she tucked an errant curl back under her snug tin hat.

She snapped the clasp of her black handbag, checked off the contents and slung it around her neck.

She was ready.

As the Liberator circled the field, several enormous bonfires came into view. Off to the left, a light flashed a discreet signal.

Heart racing, Louisa turned to Pete, the dispatcher. He shouted above the noise of the engine and wind, "If you're afraid—"

"Just give me a push," she interrupted him. *Let's get this over with.*

The firm shove in her back propelled her into freefall. A sharp tug from the line connected to the plane pulled the ripcord. Gasping at the icy touch of cold air, she fought down a panic attack, her stomach churning at the abrupt surge of the opening parachute.

Gently floating downwards, Louisa almost began to relax, only to tense again as she came closer to the ground. Would they be ambushed?

Tugging hard on the parachute cord, she tried to prevent drifting away from where she intended to land. But before she could get the parachute under control, she was unceremoniously dumped into the branches of a huge tree.

"*Mon Dieu!*" she gasped. Relief rushed through her—she was alive and unhurt. But—her heart skipped a beat—there was no sign of any welcome from her hosts, the local Maquis. *The Resistance.*

She inhaled the faint scent of smoke. Peering through the thick branches and leaves, she picked out the glow of red and yellow flames in the distance. Nearer at hand loomed the deep black shadows of hedges and trees.

A flicker of movement alerted her and she froze. Then she heard voices. Certain that a successful rendezvous was imminent, she grasped at the parachute release mechanism.

Suddenly, the sound of shots rang out. A chill gripped her, instantly stilling the movement of her hands.

Male voices barked out sharp, guttural orders. She listened in dread as she recognized the unmistakable language of the enemy—the dreaded Boche, *the Germans.*

Louisa was helpless to do anything but sit in silent witness to the attack. Had the Resistance been betrayed by a local collaborator? Had the Boche noticed both of the parachutes, or only hers? Her stomach heaved with nausea and she forced herself to draw in a deep, calming breath.

After a few minutes, the shooting stopped. Had

they captured or killed all the Frenchmen, along with her fellow agent? No doubt they were now searching for her.

Her heart thumped so loudly she was sure they'd be able to hear it. Seconds... minutes... ticked by. She lost track of time as she waited for the inevitable—the triumphant shout of recognition as the enemy spotted the parachute.

If only she hadn't landed in this damn tree! It had been impressed on all Special Operation recruits that their first priority on landing was to dispose of their parachutes. It was incriminating evidence and she was now well and truly incriminated, through sheer, rotten luck.

She drew out a revolver and waited, muscles tensed, ears alert to every sound. There were so many small noises in the countryside in the dead of night: the wind sighing through the trees, the barking of a dog and unidentifiable faint rustlings on the ground below. She couldn't hear any more voices but that was no guarantee that the enemy wasn't lying in wait for her.

Grimacing at this terrifying thought, she decided that it was either stay stuck in the tree until her lower limbs and nether regions were completely numb, or take a risk and try to climb down. Parting the branches once again, she peered through. All was still.

As far as she could tell, everyone had gone. She was alone in Normandy, separated from the people who, if all had gone according to plan, would have had her squirreled away in a safe house by now. She should be enjoying a hot meal in the company of friends and have a warm, clean bed awaiting her.

Instead, she was perched in a tree like a flustered bird that had been blown off course far away from the protection of the flock.

She'd have to survive on her own.

Tucking the revolver firmly into her coat pocket

and divesting herself of the parachute, she clung to a sturdy branch and twisted around to face the trunk. Awkwardly, she began to inch down, her best shoes slipping and slithering on the rough bark surface.

She bit her lip as she gouged her knee, smothering her gasp of pain. Darn it, she'd dressed as if she were a normal citizen just out for an evening stroll before curfew. There'd been nothing in the training about having to extricate oneself from landing in trees wearing shoes with no grip, she thought crossly.

As she dropped to the last branch, her right shoe began to slide off. Struggling to regain her balance she put all her weight onto the left foot. Her arms ached from the sudden stress of bearing the brunt of the jolt. The kitbag dragged on her shoulders.

Twisting her head to one side, she looked down to see how far she was from the ground. She would have to jump.

Suddenly, both shoes slid away, her tenuous hold gone. Cursing as her hands parted company with the rough bark, she fell heavily on top of a solid mound.

The mound moved.

And groaned.

Before she had time to react she was forcefully ejected and pitched onto her side. A heavy weight then knocked her flat on her back, one large hand covering her mouth.

"What the devil...?" The deep voice rumbled in her ears. The man looming over her appeared to be wearing a uniform. Pine needles were stuck to his collar. His face was close enough for her to feel his breath and the dark pools of his eyes glared into hers.

Stealthily, Louisa's hand crept towards her pocket.

He gave a grunt of astonishment. *"A woman?"*

She made to whip out a revolver, but he was too

quick for her. He clamped a hand on each of her wrists. She was no match for his strength.

"What are you doing here?" he demanded. His grip tightened when she didn't answer. "Who are you?"

The kitbag dug uncomfortably into her spine but she stayed silent. "What's your name?" Her mind raced. He'd spoken in English. Accent verified it was probably his first language. Even so, she hesitated. Was he friend...or foe?

Carefully keeping her tone of voice neutral so as not to give any clues as to the content of her words, she said in French, "You want to know my name? Get off me and I'll tell you." She bucked her hips sharply in an attempt to dislodge him.

Instantly, his thighs gripped her like iron and his hands tightened around her wrists. "Do you speak English?"

She didn't answer. Drawing in a breath, she repeated her offer in German. His huff of frustration told her all she needed to know—he only understood English. Heaving a sigh of relief, she indicated, with a roll of her eyes, the tree above them.

Warily, he glanced up. "Your parachute?" Before she could reply, he muttered, "I thought that unholy racket was the Jerry searching for *me*, but...it was for *you*?"

With a burst of insight, he exclaimed, "French Resistance! I've heard of people being sent in undercover to support them, but...*a female?*" He shook his head as if he couldn't believe it.

Louisa was used to this reaction from men so she simply said, "Oui." *Yes.*

He pushed himself away from her, saying in a blithe tone, "Actually, you're a Godsend. The blighters shot my Spitfire down. Maybe you can help me rejoin my squadron."

She clasped his proffered hand and found herself being firmly hauled into a standing position.

Then, in one fluid motion, she pointed her revolver at his head.

He gasped. "What?" He raised his hands in surrender. "You want proof of my identity?" He pointed to his RAF wings. "Royal Air Force."

They could be genuine...or maybe not. It was hard to see in the dark. She'd have to rely on her instincts.

She gave a brisk nod, satisfied that he was an allied airman, and stashed her gun away and stepped towards the tree.

"You want me to get the parachute down?" he suggested, plainly relieved that she'd believed him.

"S'il vous plait." *If you please.*

Leaving him to attend to this task, Louisa peeled off the overalls and tucked them under one arm. Keeping ears and eyes alert, she beckoned him to follow her over to what looked like an outline of a barn on the other side of the field. They stumbled across the lumpy ground and fell into a pile of straw just inside the opening. The barn smelled dry and was half-empty.

"Good choice," he muttered, as he threw the parachute over them both. He took the overalls she offered him and tucked them under his head. "We may as well try to get some sleep."

Louisa dragged off the tin helmet and dipped into the kitbag for her small, emerald, crushed velvet pillow. Unraveling the impact-protective bandages from her ankles she dropped them into her handbag and lay down, still wearing her coat and shoes.

The last thought to float through her mind before she fell into a fitful sleep was that this man, lying quietly beside her, was a liability which she could do without. If she had any chance at all of achieving her goals, she'd need to ditch him as soon as possible.

****

Joe woke as the first signs of light stretched across the open entrance. He groaned, his empty belly aching. It took a moment to remember where he was. The light blanket on top of him was warm and cozy. Of course—it was the girl's parachute!

She was still sleeping. Glancing at her, he was pleasantly surprised to see how young she was. Her assertive behavior had made him assume she was older. But he now saw that she was near his own age of twenty-six.

Last night, he had only seen her outline. Daylight revealed to him her pale skin and the long, black lashes brushing her cheeks. He rolled onto his side and his fingertips brushed against her tumbled ebony hair.

She looked so fragile. He wondered why such a pretty young woman would be involved in the dangerous Resistance movement? Why wasn't she safe at home, with a family of children to care for, like most girls her age? He shrugged. Maybe she just hadn't met the right bloke yet.

As he watched a sigh of breath purse her lips, a stirring of desire made him yearn to reach out and touch that smooth skin. He wanted to trail his finger down one soft cheek, to press a kiss onto... He grinned to himself. Better not get carried away. He rolled out of the straw and gently smoothed the silky parachute back against her side.

****

Louisa's eyes fluttered open. Her peripheral vision caught the outline of a man as he disappeared outside. Instantly alert, she sat up. Her head started to reel and her stomach churned with discomfort. Shakily, she pushed aside the parachute and made an effort to stand.

She staggered towards the light while pulling bits of straw out of her hair and brushing them off her crumpled clothes. A quick look around showed no sign of him. Her first thought was one of relief.

He'd gone. Maybe he felt that he'd be able to make it to safety on his own. Still, it was a pity that she didn't even get to know his name.

Half-shrugging in an effort to ease her shoulders, she turned back to the straw. Lifting a fistful, she rolled the parachute into a tight ball and stuffed it deep into the bottom of the dry stack. She piled straw back on top then reached for her bags. She grabbed the tin helmet and overalls and hid them in the same manner.

Smoothing down her skirt, straightening her stockings, brushing her hair, she tried to make herself look as though she hadn't spent the night sleeping rough. Finally, she packed away the little pillow and checked her watch. Six-thirty a.m. Time to get going.

"Good Morning!" At the sound of his voice, Louisa glanced up to see the airman's wide smile. He was holding out a loaf of bread to her. "Like some? It's still warm."

A slow blush heated her face at his sudden appearance. Quickly, she diverted her gaze to the bread.

He divided the loaf and offered her half. "I noticed a farmhouse nearby, so I knocked on the door."

"Merci." *Thank you.* Louisa, slightly bemused that he took the risk to approach strangers despite being unable to speak French, tore off a chunk and started to eat. It tasted good. She smiled.

He smiled back. "By the way, I'm Joe." He pointed to his chest as he said it and his sage-green eyes sought hers. "Joseph Fisher."

Details of his features she hadn't been able to see in the night were now clear. His eyebrows were the darkest she'd ever seen and his skin was tanned, as if he'd spent a lot of time outdoors.

It was obvious that he presumed she was French. She ought to tell him that she spoke

11

Cherie Le Clare

English. Surely it wouldn't do any harm...

"Fisher." She shook his hand. "I'm Louisa."

Surprise lit his eyes. "So you do speak English!"

"Yes," she admitted, before quickly adding, "Do you know where we are?"

"Not exactly." He produced a small cloth map from one pocket and compass from another. "But I can work it out." He combed long fingers through his short raven hair and gave her a measured look. "You'll assist me in getting back to England?"

"I'm not sure I can," she answered truthfully. The ambush meant that all her contacts were now compromised. Without them how would she be able to deliver him safely to the escape line? She sighed inwardly at the hopeful look on his face. "I'm not sure," she repeated, "but I'll do my best."

As they studied the map together, gaining their bearings and plotting their route, Louisa resolved that in the short term, she would simply concentrate on getting to where she needed to go. Meanwhile, he could come along for the ride—as long as he didn't cause any problems.

Louisa wiped the crumbs from her mouth, looped her handbag over her arm and started to hoist the kitbag.

He reached out towards it. "Let me carry that for you; it must be heavy."

She hesitated for only an instant, appreciating his gallant gesture. "Thanks."

He grinned and took it from her, slinging it easily over one shoulder.

"We'd better get going," she said. "It's a long walk to Paris." She moved towards the doorway and scanned the area before motioning him to follow her. They headed out into the grey dawn light and swiftly made their way across the open field, slipping into the thicket of trees and making their way towards the sound of running water.

She stifled a curse as small bushes and twigs

snagged her silk stockings. A glance at Fisher showed his boots glistening with dew.

They scrambled their way down a short bank. Louisa slipped on the loose soil and Fisher turned, offering his hand to steady her. At the stream's edge, she hunched down, cupped the cool water in her hands and sniffed. It smelled fresh and she gulped it down. She scooped up another handful to wash her face before signaling she was going to duck behind a bush to relieve herself.

Her mind wandered as she recalled Fisher's courteous gesture and the strength in his warm grip, only moments ago.

About to emerge, a sound nearby made her scalp tingle.

Footsteps.

Pulse hammering, she stepped out and glanced at the airman, who quickly headed into the thicket to hide.

A raised voice in the still air caused a sudden flapping of wings as birds scattered.

Louisa twisted around to meet the cold, steely glare of two high-booted German soldiers. Were they looking for her? Trying to appear as though merely out for an innocent early morning stroll, she faced them squarely, greeting them with a cool "Bonjour." *Good day*.

"Bonjour mademoiselle." *Good day miss*. "What are you doing out so early in the morning?"

Louisa thought quickly. "I was taking my little dog for a walk but she's run ahead. Have you seen her?"

Ignoring this, the taller of the two asked, "Have you noticed any strangers around?"

"Strangers?"

With an edge of impatience in his tone, the shorter one intervened. "British airmen!"

Louisa shrugged. "Non." *No*.

Relieved that they were not looking for members

of the Resistance, she smiled, hoping to distract them from their search. She needed to keep them talking, to divert their attention somehow.

She was totally unprepared for what happened next. One of the soldiers cried out as he pointed over her shoulder. She whirled around. *Oh, no!* He'd spotted the airman trying to cross from the thicket to the forest.

Why hadn't he stayed hidden? Desperately, Louisa followed the men as they gave chase. But she didn't have a hope of keeping up. The last thing she saw was the soldiers gaining on Fisher and forcing him into a car that was parked in a clearing.

Stopping to catch her breath, she could only watch helplessly as the vehicle carried him—and her kitbag of vital supplies—away.

Chapter Two

Joe, restrained in the back seat, fought the desire to glance through the window. He didn't want to alert his captors to any connection between him and the girl.

He sucked in a deep breath and considered the situation. He hadn't actually counted on being caught. But now that he was in the enemy's clutches, he inwardly winced at his impulsiveness. It was too late for regrets, but at least he'd succeeded in distracting them from Louisa.

He glanced to his side at the fair-haired guard's profile. There was a light fuzz of hair above his top lip. He was only a boy—Joe estimated about eighteen years old.

"Where are you taking me?"

The youth shrugged. "Ich habe nicht verstanden." *I don't understand.*

They came to a screeching halt outside an old stone farm house. After being hurriedly escorted into a little room off the inner courtyard, Joe was directed to sit on a wooden chair against the wall. The young soldier followed him, shut the timber door behind them and stood stiffly to attention.

Joe could sense the boy's eyes on him as he checked out the humble dirt floor, the cobweb-laced window frame and the dirt-smudged glass. The only escape route was through the door.

Joe sat back, casually running his hand through a drooping lock of hair. From his top pocket he drew out a tin of tobacco. He glanced up to see the boy leaning forward, a flicker of interest on his face. Joe spread a pinch of tobacco into the paper, carefully rolled it together then touched the little package to his lips. As his tongue slipped backward and forward to seal it, he watched the guard following every move. Pinching the ends together, he raised the completed cigarette to his nose and inhaled appreciatively.

He held the cigarette out, gesturing to the youth to take it. The guard smiled. As he stretched forward, Joe stood up and shoved him hard against the wall. The boy's smile faded as Joe lifted a fist and slammed it against the astonished boy's chin.

"Sorry about that, mate," he muttered as the boy slid, unconscious, to the floor. Cautiously opening the door, Joe sprinted across the deserted yard.

****

Louisa rushed back to the farmhouse where Fisher had been given the bread and lifted the knocker.

The door opened a crack and a pair of black button eyes in a crinkled, sunbrowned face peeked around the edge.

"Bonjour, Madame. Can you help me, s'il vous plait? Where is the nearest Boche command post?" Louisa, heart pumping, sucked in a shallow breath.

The old lady blinked and called to someone over her shoulder. A brutish, middle-aged man appeared, demanding gruffly, "Why do you want to know?"

Louisa hesitated. What if these people were Nazi sympathizers and, after giving Fisher the bread, had tipped off the local guard about him?

She smiled to put them at ease. "I have a message for the Guard Commander. Alas, as you can see," she indicated the disheveled state of her stockings, "I fell off my bicycle. I've been walking but am now a little lost. Can you help?"

The man's whole demeanor changed as, pushing himself forward, he said politely, "Mademoiselle, it will be my pleasure to take you."

He led her to a parked truck and opened the

door for her to get in. Grateful that her ruse had worked, she silently prayed that she'd made the right choice. She wasn't at all certain just how, or if, she could help the airman. But, even if she couldn't do anything for him, he had taken her kitbag and she was determined to try and recover it.

"How far is it?"

"A little way," rasped the driver as the vehicle crawled along the road.

After ten minutes, Louisa craned forward to check their progress through the windscreen. "Are we almost there?"

He didn't answer.

The hair rose on the back of her neck at his silence. She stole a glance at him. His eyes glowed with unnerving intensity and there was a leering half-smile on his face. Her stomach clenched. Swallowing hard, she inwardly cursed that she'd been put into this position. Maybe she should have let Fisher take his chances and to hell with trying to rescue him from the hole he'd deliberately dug. It was probably hopeless anyway—what could she do?

Her throat dried and her chest tightened painfully. Gripping the sides of the seat, she commanded, "Stop, s'il vous plaît! I'll find my own way from here."

The driver's lip curled and he yanked the steering wheel, flinging Louisa against the door. The truck stopped and the decrepit door flew open, spilling her onto the ground. She winced as her left ankle turned. Limping, she tried to run towards the trees. As heavy boots closed in on her, she jerked out a revolver.

Two beefy arms circled her waist, capturing her back against his chest in a vise-like grip. She kicked out and bucked against him but he knocked her forward, slamming her face-down into the grass. Snatching her revolver, he tossed it into the trees and then grabbed her arms, forcing them behind her waist. She grunted, twisting uncomfortably as he tied her wrists together with something scratchy, like twine.

"Let me go!" Louisa shrilled, outraged. Her spare revolver was now out of reach, and she had no way to defend herself. He pressed his stout belly against her spine and she shuddered as he rasped in her ear, "A sweet flower is ripe for ze picking—oui?" A calloused hand slid up her skirt.

"No!" Louisa's skin crawled at his touch. "Get away from me!" As his hot hand groped at the tender, exposed skin above her suspenders, she screamed. And screamed louder. Forced into silence as her head was yanked back by a twist of her hair, she stared into the forest. Her eyes widened. Someone was there.

It was Fisher. He'd stooped to pick up her revolver.

Her heart leapt, and as a foul, hot breath fanned her forehead, Louisa rolled her eyes upward. Had the oafish brute spotted the airman?

He pressed her face back into the dry grass. She spat grit, her stomach heaving with revulsion. *Hurry up Fisher, help me, now!*

A shot rang out. Her assailant twisted away from her. As a second shot whistled dangerously close to her head, she heard him running towards the road. She glanced up just as he turned back to snatch her dislodged handbag.

She cried out as the oaf ran towards his truck then heard a yell of pain as the second shot found its mark. Dumping her bag, he leapt into the truck and revved the motor. Only a flesh wound then. *Damn.*

As the vehicle sped away, the airman's final bullet ricocheted off the metal door. Quickly, he fetched the bag and crouched to untie Louisa's wrists. She pushed herself up from the ground and knelt to face him.

"Did he hurt you?" he asked.

"No, I'm fine." Though trembling with shock, she briskly dismissed the question of her welfare, turning instead to her handbag and peering inside. "You've saved me a journey. I was just on my way to rescue you."

He smiled. "You were?"

She nodded. "Thought you might want some assistance."

"I don't think I was the one who needed help," Fisher pointed out. He indicated her bag. "Did he...?"

Louisa closed the bag with a snap.

"What's missing?" He pulled her to her feet.

She shook her head. "He didn't get his grubby hands on my francs, thank God. They're for the Resistance." Rubbing her bruised wrists, she sent him a grateful look as he passed the revolver to her. "How did you find your way...?"

"Your screams were enough to wake the dead. I couldn't resist a damsel in distress now, could I?" His self-mocking smile gave way to a stern frown. "You really must be more careful about hitching rides with strangers."

Louisa hissed in a breath and hit out at Joe's arm. But his reflexes were too quick for her and he sidestepped, neatly avoiding her glancing blow. He turned back to her with a maddening smirk.

Her fingers twitched as she glared at him. "You dare to rebuke *me*?" Her voice shook with all the suppressed tension of the past hours. "It's entirely *your* fault I got into this mess in the first place!"

She glanced into the trees. Had he been followed? The area was sure to be thoroughly searched.

Jamming the revolver into her pocket and tugging the kitbag from Joe's shoulders, she strode away, cursing under her breath at the sharp stab in her ankle.

Still fuming as he easily caught up to her, she

stifled a groan at their recent lost opportunity—if Fisher's aim had been fatal, things could have been very different.

He appeared to guess her thoughts. "I didn't want any bullets to hit you by mistake. Hell, I'm sorry, Louisa, we could've taken his truck."

"Yes," she snapped. "And exchanged your uniform for his clothing."

He frowned. "It was bloody daft of me to try to divert those soldiers this morning, but I didn't want you to be captured—I've heard what they do to female prisoners, and if they'd discovered that you speak English..."

She sucked in her lip. They both faced the possibility of arrest, imprisonment, torture...and this was all the more likely if the airman acted on impulse again. She'd have to convince him that they must work as a team. She glanced at his anxious face. He'd had the grace to apologize. She should let him know she wouldn't hold a grudge.

"You meant well," she conceded softly.

They trudged together in silence. Louisa, however, couldn't keep up the swift pace for long and was soon trailing well behind him.

****

Joe stopped and looked back over his shoulder as he waited for her to catch up. He could see that she was favoring one leg and walking with difficulty.

He jogged back to her. One glance at her face showed the pain she was in.

"I landed badly when I fell from that truck," she explained, her breath short. As he drew level, he offered her his arm. She clasped it tightly.

Adjusting his stride to suit, he could feel the effort it was costing her in each step she took. And yet she hadn't once complained. He guessed that she'd continue on even if it half-killed her.

"Let's stop for a rest. This seems as good a place as any." He looked around and pointed to the small rise ahead of them. "Come on, old girl, race you to the top."

He smiled at her amused hoot of laughter. It was the bonniest sound he'd ever heard.

****

It was a good place to stop, Louisa thought. From where they sat, they could see for miles and observe if anyone approached. The sun was high, cooled by a stirring breeze. Resting her throbbing ankle on top of her velvet pillow, she secretly admired the airman's broad shoulders as he stood, his back to her, surveying the fields and roads below.

Supporting herself by her elbows, she laid back on his jacket, which he'd placed onto the ground for her. Captured body warmth flowed through into her limbs. Grateful for the chance to relax, she called softly, "Hey, Airman Fisher—"

"Joe...please...call me Joe," he interrupted, turning to face her.

She smiled. "Thanks...Joe."

He walked towards her, puzzled. "For what?"

"For being in the right place at the right time... you saved my reputation back there."

Joe pulled a rueful face as he sank down beside her. "No need to thank me."

She reached into her coat, withdrew a revolver and laid it beside him. "You may require this again." In answer to his querying look, she added, "I have a spare."

Joe gave her an appreciative glance. He tucked the gun into his belt and quietly said, "Bless you. I lost mine in the plane crash."

Louisa smiled, pleased with his reaction. They could now equally share the responsibility for one another's safety; at least that was her intention. She hoped he understood that.

Straightening up, she turned to face him. "You haven't told me how you escaped?"

"I introduced one baby-faced guard to my fist."

He offered his bruised knuckles for her inspection. "Then I ran for it. Luckily, the rest of the blighters were busily occupied with dinner... or something." He grinned. "Which reminds me..." Joe reached for her kitbag and started rummaging through it. "Any kai in here? I don't know about you, but I'm starving."

A memory flashed before Louisa's eyes, startling her. She clutched her heart. "*Kai?*"

Joe glanced up, surprised. "It's a Maori word—it means food, in my country."

Regretting her over-reaction and anxious to avoid any awkward questions from him, she quickly asked, "You're a New Zealander?"

"Yep," he agreed. "A kiwi, born and bred." He resumed exploring her kitbag, triumphantly extracting a bar of the very best Belgian chocolate. His eyes widened.

"You beauty!" Breaking it in half, he turned to offer it to her. "How on earth did you get this on your food ration?"

Louisa merely smiled and put the chocolate to her lips. He wasn't to know that it was one of the perks of being a Special Op's agent. As she bit into the sweetly smooth substance, he winked flirtatiously.

A bubble of laughter burst from her throat. Joe was a cocky so-and-so but she couldn't help warming to him.

It was obvious that he was enjoying it too. Some sweet food in their stomachs had lifted both their moods. He snapped off another piece and said, "What about you? Where do you call home?"

"We moved around a lot when I was growing up. My father is French, my mother, English." She shrugged. "But, until recently, I had an apartment in Paris."

Joe smiled. "I've heard it's a beautiful city." He started foraging through her kitbag again. "My stomach still feels as though my throat's been cut."

"I'm hungry, too," she agreed, with a wry grin at his graphic kiwi metaphor. "We'll need to get a hot meal inside us before we go much further." She winced as she lifted her ankle off the pillow.

He ceased his search and turned his attention to her foot. "This shoe ought to come off to ease that swelling." He glanced at her with a questioning look.

"No, I'll never be able to get it on again. Just help me up, will you, please?"

She wobbled as she put all her balance onto the good foot. As her other foot brushed the ground, she bit her lip so hard that she drew a drop of blood. She could cope with physical pain, but something in Joe's expression opened a barely sealed wound deep inside her.

Sorrow swelled her throat. She started to turn away, but stopped when he raised a finger to her lips to dab at the cut.

She stared, transfixed, as he lifted his finger from her mouth and into his own.

His gaze locked onto hers and slowly, *sensually*, he withdrew his finger, cleansing it of her blood.

Louisa's cheeks warmed. She wasn't sure whether she was appalled or thrilled.

But...one thing she was sure of. She had never before met any man quite so...so *naughty*.

A tingle of yearning rippled through her. She ached to feel his lips on hers. Shocked at her response, she took a step backwards, cursing aloud as her ankle throbbed anew.

He frowned. "You're in too much pain to walk any further. Maybe I should try and find someone to help."

"But you don't speak French..."

He swore softly and said, "That shoe really will have to come off. The ankle needs strapping up."

"I have bandages." She opened her handbag.

If he'd noticed that she'd agreed without

argument, he made no sign of it. While she sat to unstrap her shoe, he found the bandages, crouched beside her and began to wrap the ankle in a figure eight pattern. "Comfortable?"

She nodded. "Thanks."

He sat back as if to survey his handiwork, one hand stroking the line of his chin. "Back in a minute." Picking up his jacket, he headed off into the trees and quickly returned with a branch.

Using it to balance herself, she hopped a couple of steps forward. Glancing back with a smile, she said, "Let's get going. We'll need to find food and shelter before nightfall."

Gathering up her things, she hobbled beside him as they inched their way down the grassy slope towards the road below.

****

Joe's arm began to ache. Louisa was relying on him to keep herself balanced and moving. He didn't begrudge it. Casting a quick sideways glance, he noted the beads of sweat forming on her upper lip and brow. She was bravely struggling along, but he knew that there was a limit to how far they would get this afternoon. She was exhausted.

****

"Over there!" Louisa pointed. "Look, there's a village." She glanced at him as he reached for his map. "You could change your clothes and boots there, if we can find someone to take us in."

They moved forward, picking up a little pace as they sensed an end to their journey. Louisa fancied that she could even smell a meal cooking.

The road was quiet as they made their way along. It was really little more than a country lane, rutted with deep potholes and tire tracks.

Louisa was so busy concentrating on every step that she didn't hear the bicycle until it was right beside them. The elderly cyclist, a beret perched jauntily on his head, called out to them as he slowly pedalled past.

"Merde!" Louisa stopped.

Joe shot her a sharp look. "Trouble?"

Her pulse jumped. "There's a patrol coming through."

Catching his anxiety, she sucked in her top lip. How far away were they? Would she and Joe have enough time to find shelter? Hastily drawing in a dry, shuddering breath, she glanced over her shoulder.

****

Joe could see nowhere for them to hide. Pulling away from her, he ran towards the nearby sound of a barking dog. As he rounded the bend, he saw a cottage with a mongrel chained up outside.

Heart pounding, he ran back to Louisa. He bent down and, in one swift movement, swept her up in his arms and headed for the building. Struggling along the rough path, he staggered onto the porch. The mongrel's barks quietened to a whimper.

He put his shoulder to the door and it swung open. He set Louisa gently onto her feet and paused briefly to catch his breath. He closed the door behind them, alert for any occupants.

The house was silent.

Louisa slumped down, exhausted, onto a wooden chair.

Joe glanced at the cream plastered walls, smothered in dusty, framed prints. Reaching to trail the tips of his fingers over the ceiling's low, stained timber beams, he strode to the narrow staircase. It led to a sleeping loft directly above the fireplace. Nobody was home.

He crossed to a window. Pushing aside the frilly lace curtains, he checked for any sign of the patrol. All he saw was a handkerchief lying on the path. It must have dropped out of Louisa's pocket.

He flopped down onto the armchair next to her. Easing off his uncomfortably warm boots, Joe leaned

forward to massage his feet.
The dog started barking again.
A tingle of fear crawled along his spine.

Chapter Three

"Dickie!"

Joe's head shot up at the familiarity in Louisa's voice. Who the hell was Dickie?

A sandy-haired man, sporting an immense handlebar moustache and dressed in a white and grey striped shirt, braces securing his trousers, emerged from a back room.

He ran to embrace Louisa, greeting her with a British upper class accent. "Lulu...darling! How did you wash up here?"

"How did you?" Louisa countered, returning his hug with gusto. "I...I thought you were dead!"

The man grinned. "It'll take more than a few Boche to put the kibosh on me..."

"I can't believe our luck!" Louisa laughed, shaking her head in obvious amazement. "*Mon Dieu*...Who would have dreamed that we'd bump into each other at this cottage?" After a moment, she gestured to Joe and said, "Dickie, this is Joe Fisher. His plane was shot down."

"Found us a customer already? That was quick work." Dickie shook Joe's hand. "Pleased to meet you, old chap."

Just as Joe began to measure the feeling of this greeting—he could tell a lot about a person from their handshake—a huge ruckus started up outside. The dog was now yapping furiously and there was the sound of raised voices.

Dickie indicated the back door. "Quick, beat it!"

Joe didn't wait to be told twice. He threw a quick glance at Louisa and she nodded curtly as if to indicate that she would be okay. Then he sprinted down the hallway and, heart hammering, opened the door to the outside yard.

A quick glance around revealed only one place, an open shed, which he immediately rejected as being too obvious. His heart sank. Then, to the right of the door, he noticed a very large, wooden rainwater barrel. Taking the lid off, he peered in. It was about two thirds full. It might just do, if he hunkered down. He lowered himself into the chilly water and eased the lid over. Squatting in the darkness, he shivered and prepared himself for a long, damp wait.

His air force boots! He'd left them inside! Silently cursing, he fought to keep calm. There was nothing he could do about it now, but he'd not forgive himself if, as a result of this carelessness, Louisa was harmed. Tense as a coiled spring, his temples began to throb with a slow, dull ache.

****

Louisa stood up, shoved the kitbag onto the chair seat and sat back down. She arranged the folds of her coat to appear as though she were sitting on a pillow. Folding her hands into her lap in a vain attempt to calm the butterflies doing cartwheels in her stomach, she watched as Dickie opened the door and shouted at the dog to be quiet.

A German officer and two rank and file soldiers were standing on the step. The officer seemed preoccupied with examining what looked like a small square of grubby white material. He showed it to his men and she heard them discussing it. Just as she began to wonder why a dirty rag could be of such interest to them, she saw Dickie snatch the opportunity to make a visual check of the room.

She saw his eyes widen at something he'd seen. Alerted, she looked in the direction of his stare. *Merde!*

Butterflies now jumping wildly she quietly edged her good foot over towards Joe's boots. If she could reach them she'd push them under her chair, where they'd be out of sight. Her shoe touched one boot and she swiveled around a little so that she could nudge them both. Slowly, surely, she inched them closer to her while keeping watch on the group at the door. Fortunately, they seemed totally distracted by Dickie, who was fielding questions from the officer.

Her own knowledge of German vocabulary was pretty basic. Nevertheless, she understood that the rag appeared to be a map. *Mon Dieu!* It must be Joe's. No wonder they were so interested in it.

Desperate to hide the boots, she fought to keep her balance. Her scalp prickled with perspiration and her coat felt unbearably hot.

The officer seemed to become agitated. She could tell from his tone and narrowed eyes that he had lost patience.

One final jerk and she pushed the boots home.

"Heraus!" The officer pushed Dickie aside, gesturing to the soldiers to search the place. They strode in, casting smirks in Louisa's direction.

She shrugged herself out of her coat, letting it slip down further over the legs of her chair. Then, folding one leg over the other, she smiled up at them demurely from under her lashes.

The officer glanced at her bandaged foot. "Vot is this?"

Louisa flashed him a smile. "A sprained ankle, sir. I twisted it in a hole." She winked slowly. "I was being chased by a very bad man."

The officer's lips twitched in brief amusement. He motioned his men to check out the loft and back kitchen. Turning away from Louisa, he was examining the inside of the fireplace chimney when his men came back in.

"Outside yard!" he barked.

Louisa held her breath.

Dickie sat down on a low table, draped with a

mauve cloth. He put his hand on her arm as if he thought she might be tempted to try and stop them.

He need not have worried. She knew only too well that there was nothing she could do. She consoled herself with the thought that Joe had had enough time to make himself scarce.

Seconds ticked by.

A shout from one of the men caught the officer's attention.

Louisa braced herself.

The officer motioned Dickie ahead of him. Louisa, finding herself ignored, watched them both hurry out. She hobbled her way after them, her limbs heavy with anxiety. As Louisa reached the open doorway, she jumped at the sound of a terrified squeal followed by a gunshot.

Please God, no.

Dickie and the officer were standing beside a rough stone outbuilding. She watched a stream of blood oozing, drip by drip, onto the cobbles as the men dragged...Sickened, she closed her eyes.

Poor Joe.

"Lulu. It's fine, darling. They've found something more valuable," Dickie murmured as he walked towards her.

Her eyes snapped open. "What...what do you mean?"

"Fresh pork," he joked, adding in a graver tone, "They've now moved on to search the neighbor's place. It looks as if Fisher has scarpered. With any luck, he's holed up somewhere safe."

The sense of relief overwhelmed her. She threw her arms around him in a hug.

"Hey, steady on!" Dickie exclaimed. Then he hugged her back.

****

Joe's skin prickled with relief as he heard Dickie's and Louisa's voices. After that unholy commotion he'd been expecting the worst. About to reveal his hiding place, he suddenly hesitated. They were speaking in French—he had no idea what they were saying. Deciding that it would be prudent to stay until he was certain that it was safe to clamber out, he stifled a sneeze and resigned himself for a long wait.

****

"Thank God they didn't discover the radio set," Dickie said, heading for the kitchen. "It would have been a disaster if they had." He reached for the kettle. "We'll have a cup of tea and you can tell me how you came to injure that ankle."

"Never mind that!" Louisa frowned with exasperation. "What about Joe? We can't just forget about him. And anyway, how did you escape that attack last night? As far as I could tell, everyone but me was taken."

Dickie, offering the kettle to Louisa, said firmly, "Tea first. Talk later. You'll find the water outside." Glancing at her foot, he appeared to change his mind. "No, perhaps—"

"I'll manage, thanks," Louisa interrupted, taking hold of the kettle. She couldn't let him believe that she was an invalid. He just might take it upon himself to cut her out of the action, and that would be unbearable.

Dickie pursed his lips but let her have her way.

It was only a couple of steps out to the barrel but it was enough to renew the throbbing. She wondered when, or if, she'd ever get to see Joe again and inwardly winced as the pain of that thought hit her harder than the tenderness of her foot.

Grasping the lid of the barrel, she pushed it to one side.

"Mon Dieu!"

Joe grinned. "You sure are a sight for sore eyes."

Unfurling like a moth emerging from a chrysalis, he heaved himself out. Dripping water formed puddles at his feet. He stretched his limbs and glanced at the kettle. "I'm ready for a cuppa."

Gazing into his face as if she'd never seen it before, she noticed the way his smile crinkled the skin at the corners of his eyes.

He lifted a cold, wet hand to stroke a wisp of hair away from her cheek.

"Joe Fisher," she murmured quietly, "You must have the luck of the Irish."

"Devil, more like." His gaze skimmed her face. "Are you all right?"

"I think so." Smiling, she squeezed his hand.

Dickie called, "What's the hold-up, Lulu?"

As they moved indoors, she answered teasingly, "I've just found the biggest drowned rat you've ever..."

Dickie raised his eyebrows then burst into laughter when he saw Joe. "Of all the places... no wonder they didn't find you! It wouldn't occur to them to look into a barrel of water."

Joe grinned. "The buggers walked right past me."

Clapping his hands together decisively, Dickie said, "Right, now that we're all present and accounted for, I'm off to the village to get you some clothes. What size shoe are you?" He stared at Joe's sodden feet. "Good Lord! Could be a little tricky finding a pair in your size, old chap."

Louisa groaned, carefully lowering herself onto a nearby stool. "Forget the tea. I need a proper drink— preferably one that's an anesthetic." She indicated the nearest cupboard. "Got anything stashed away in here?"

Dickie reached into the cupboard and produced a flask of cider. "Best I can do. Oh, and there's some bread and cheese in the pantry—should be some eggs left as well."

Joe started to peel off his wet socks. "We'll have a meal ready for you when you get back—pity about the bacon."

"Ha—hope it chokes 'em." Dickie scowled as he headed for the door.

"Here." Joe pushed a box towards Louisa and gently lifted her injured leg onto it. He'd now stripped down to his waist, dominating the small space with his masculinity.

Louisa grew warm as she caught the movement of his arm muscles and the curls of dark hair across his upper chest.

Pulling two mugs over and filling them with cider, she took a long, satisfying sip. It seemed a long time since a drink had tasted so good.

Joe had found an old towel to wrap around himself. He moved to the sink to wring the water from his sodden clothes. He hadn't dried himself properly. Delicate drops of water shone on his back and legs.

"I thought they'd be sure to notice my boots." Joe draped his jacket and trousers over the backs of two chairs. "But seems they overlooked them."

"It was your map they were more interested in."

"What? But I didn't..." He turned the pockets of his jacket inside out but they were empty. "Damn and blast! Must've dropped out somehow."

Louisa handed him a mug. As he took it from her, their fingers touched and she trembled with a rush of excitement.

"Cheers!" He touched his mug to hers. "Here's to freedom!"

By the time they'd had a few more rounds of cider, they'd forgotten all about the food. Joe assisted Louisa to a back bedroom. There was only one bed. She watched with gratitude as Joe fetched her kitbag and coat. As he left the room, he announced over his shoulder, "You get some rest. I'll keep watch till Dickie returns."

Louisa stripped down to her underwear, placed the revolver under the pillow and snuggled down under the covers.

She awoke some time later to a darkened room lit only by the moonlight shining through the uncurtained window. It took her a moment to remember where she was.

Sitting up, she swung her legs onto the floor and tested her ankle. Stooping to unwind the bandage, she pressed the tender spot with her fingers. The swelling was almost gone and there was only a slight twinge of pain.

Relieved to be almost back to her former self, she looked around for her clothes. They were stacked on the chair where she'd left them. Glancing at the small table beside the bed, she saw a plate with a piece of cake on it.

How did that get there? She rubbed her eyes, convinced that she must be seeing things. Cakes were rare since the war began—rationing had ensured that. On closer inspection, it turned out to be a cheese sandwich. *Good old Joe.* She munched it quickly, suddenly realizing how hungry she was. It was a good starter, but her stomach was growling for more.

After retrieving her revolver and pulling her coat on over her underwear, she opened the door. The house seemed very quiet. She paused, listening carefully, but there was no sound. The boys must be asleep. Slipping the gun into her pocket, she padded her way across to the dark kitchen and dragged aside the window curtain.

She turned on the tap, grimacing at the rusty colored liquid dribbling out. No wonder Dickie had preferred the rainwater. She filled the saucepan from the kettle and put it on the stove to boil. She popped in two eggs.

Picking up a torn scrap of newspaper, she settled herself down on the stool to read. "What the...?" She hadn't realized she'd spoken aloud until a figure loomed in the doorway.

"You're feeling better?" Joe, briskly rubbing his

hands through his hair, stepped into the kitchen. Without waiting for an answer, he gestured towards the paper. "What's that?"

"Good question." She handed it to him. "Take a look." She noticed that he was still wearing only the towel. Obviously Dickie had not yet returned with the promised clothes.

He squinted. "Can't see it properly. Why don't we put the light on?" He leaned across as if about to close the curtains.

"No." She put a hand on his arm. "Please don't. I like the moonlight."

He gave her a surprised look, but did as she requested.

She pointed to the scrap of paper. "It's from a German newspaper, *Die Wacht Am* something or other."

"I wonder how it got here?" Joe said, passing it back to her.

"More to the point—why?" She turned the heat down a little as the water began to bubble in the pot. She flicked her wrist. "Damn. I left my watch beside the bed. What's the time, please?"

Joe consulted the luminous dial on his watch. "It's twenty-three sixteen, about right for a midnight snack." He raised a questioning eyebrow. "Three minutes for the eggs?"

"Yes, that'll do." Louisa studied the scrap of paper again. "It's just filthy propaganda."

"Can you understand what it says?" Joe asked.

"Some." She peered at it more closely. "This is about 'Our Noble Fuhrer.' And what a great leader he is. Shoddy printing, though."

"Don't know how you can read it in this weak light," Joe grumbled. "Let alone analyze it. You were a teacher before the war, I presume?"

"You presume wrong." Louisa pulled a face. "Teacher? Heaven forbid."

"What's wrong with being a teacher? It's a very

noble profession."

"So's nursing, but I wasn't one of those, either. I suppose you'll now assume that I was either a secretary or shop assistant." She bent forward and repeatedly tapped the edge of one hand against the hard bench.

"Um, well, it is traditional for girls…" Joe's voice trailed off as he watched her. "What are you doing?"

She paused to examine her hand. "I'm hardening it up." Resuming the action, she explained, "I've never been the same as other girls, Joe, not before the war and certainly not now. The saboteur training for this assignment was the hardest thing I've ever done—and I was the only female in the course. If necessary, I could kill a man with this hand." She held his gaze. "I'm no helpless little woman, Joe."

He raised one eyebrow. "I'm starting to realize that." Then he added dryly, "Still, you weren't much of a match against that brute who attacked you. He was a lot bigger."

As an awkward silence fell, Louisa cursed inwardly. Did he think her reckless? Damn it, she didn't need his approval. They barely knew each other. She had a valid reason for the choice she'd made and she didn't have to justify it to him.

Joe eyed the paper. "I reckon that's just a piece of old fish and chip wrapping." He hitched his towel more firmly around his waist and sighed wistfully. "What I wouldn't give for a good feed of that right now."

Louisa snorted and tossed the newspaper back where she'd found it. "Fish and chips? Be serious. This is France, remember?" Lifting the pot from the stove, she reached for a dish to slide the eggs onto. "You'll just have to make do with one of these."

****

As they ate, Joe thought about what she'd said. He was intrigued as to why such a feminine girl would act so tough. Her hair tumbled prettily around her shoulders and, in the moon's light, her eyes gleamed cat-like. But, claws aside, he suspected that there was a lovely softness hidden under the fiery exterior. He knew he was certainly tempted to find out.

****

Louisa finished eating and stood to wash at the sink. She swilled water around her mouth and splashed more over her face, closing her eyes at the refreshing feel. Fully engrossed in her task she stretched an arm out across the bench to grope for a towel. Instead, her fingers touched smooth skin.

"Looking for this?"

Her eyes flew open at the sound of Joe's teasing tone. She blinked, her face heating as he indicated the towel around his waist. Indignantly, she remarked, "Where the hell has Dickie got to? He should have been back with some clothing for you ages ago!"

"Never mind him."

Louisa fell silent as Joe unwound a corner of the towel, deftly retaining his modesty as he patted her face dry. His gentle, considerate touch was like a caress. Pleasure flickered through her as she murmured her thanks.

He moved closer, so close she could feel his warmth enveloping her.

She lifted her chin. His lips found hers. It was merely a touch, a light sweep of softness.

"You shouldn't have done that," she sighed, yet she hadn't drawn back in refusal.

At the same moment, a draught of air cooled her skin. She glanced down to see that the unbuttoned flaps of her coat had parted, exposing the ghastly woollen underwear which HQ had insisted was de rigueur for all Frenchwomen these days. Her face reddened but as she was about to draw the flaps together, he firmly gripped her wrist.

"Don't move," he commanded, softly.

A murmur of protest died on her lips as Joe stared at something over her shoulder. She chanced a backward glance.

Someone was watching them through the window.

Chapter Four

Joe grabbed his jacket and revolver, wrenched open the back door and disappeared into the night.

Louisa heard male voices. Joe must have caught the intruder. But what reason would anyone have for breaking the curfew? A cloud blocked the thin moonlight at the window. She eased the gun from her coat and inched her way along the wall until she bumped into the doorframe. She called out, "Joe!"

No answer.

She flicked the light switch. With one hand shielding her eyes against the glare, she edged her way into the hallway.

No one was there.

"What's going on?" she shouted.

"Lou, watch out!"

Her pulse leapt as she spied a distorted shadow on the opposite wall. "I know someone's there," she said in French, keeping her voice calm. "Reveal yourself, whoever you are." She waited, scarcely daring to breathe. She watched the shadow move ominously closer as a figure began to sidle along the wall. She yelled, "Arret!" *Halt!*

The man hesitated.

Joe staggered in, both hands covering his nose.

The stranger started to twist around. Louisa, in two short strides, closed the gap between them. Placing the gun at his back, she demanded, "State your business!"

He remained silent. She raised the gun to his head.

"Shoot not!" he pleaded. "I am looking for M'sieur Dupont, s'il vous plait."

She glanced at Joe, interpreting, "That's Dickie." She turned her attention back to the man. "What do you want with him?"

"I've heard that 'e may, mm, 'elp people."

Louisa narrowed her eyes. She would need to handle this carefully. It could be a trap.

"Are you Jewish, or someone you know is...?"

He stiffened but remained silent.

"I don't have time to play games," she growled. "If you are genuinely looking for M'sieur Dupont, then yes, you have come to the right place. But if you are here to cause trouble, then be assured, I will have no hesitation in shooting you."

"Non, please, I, mm, my...wife is...Jewish."

Allowing him to turn to face her, she completed a brisk reconnaissance of the man: short, brown hair mostly hidden under a large, flat cap, neatly trimmed beard, wiry body. Without taking her gaze off him, she gestured to Joe. "Search him for me, will you?" As Joe moved forward, Louisa blanched at the large splotches of blood on Joe's jacket and towel.

Catching Louisa's expression, he said, "He swung a punch at me." Completing the frisk, Joe extracted the man's identity card and handed it to her.

"Alain Pelet. Aged thirty-eight," she read aloud.

"Oui, Mademoiselle." Anxious brown eyes sought hers. "Please, it is urgent...M'sieur Dupont, 'e can 'elp Colette?" He broke off with a look of desperation as, from outside, the dog began to whimper.

Who could blame him for being so frightened, she thought, with all Jewish citizens being persecuted and under constant threat of deportation to God knows where. Fully expecting to see Dickie at the door, she gestured to M'sieur Pelet to sit. "Don't move," she instructed.

She opened the door, her eyes widening with surprise as she looked down to see a young child of about four years old patting the dog.

"Ah oui, Mimi!" Alain exclaimed. "What are you doing 'ere?"

Louisa snatched the child inside and shut the door.

The girl ran to her father. "Papa…"

"This is my youngest daughter," he explained, frowning at the round-eyed Mimi. "You shouldn't 'ave followed me. You were to stay with the others." To Louisa, he said, "Ah, oui. She's too little to, mm, realize the danger."

Louisa raised an eyebrow. "There are others?"

Alain sighed and moved to the door, Mimi in tow. Pausing on the step, he pursed his lips and whistled.

Louisa's pulse raced. Was it a signal for an attack? Her fingers tightened on the revolver. Could he really be prepared to gamble with his child's safety?

Alain stood aside as a woman, holding tight to the hands of a boy and a girl aged about nine or ten, emerged hesitantly from the dark.

Pocketing the revolver, Louisa ushered the family in. Firmly securing the door against the night, she prayed that she had done the right thing. She reminded herself that they could have been set up as decoys and the house could be under surveillance right now. Hastily, she double-checked the locks. Even if the family was genuine, their safety depended on Dickie having the contacts to move them on…Her heart sank. Where was he? The longer these visitors stayed, the more danger everyone was in.

****

Louisa stretched her cramped limbs in the chair in which she had spent the remainder of the night. Rubbing the back of her neck in an attempt to ease the stiffness, she listened to the snuffles from the sleeping family in the loft. Daylight now filtered in under the curtains and Dickie still had not returned.

Maybe he'd decided to wait till curfew was over before making his way back. Yes, that would make sense. She pushed aside the other thought, the disturbing one—*What if he ran into trouble?*

She sniffed the air. Was that the aroma of fried bread? That was just the pick-me-up she needed— she never could think on an empty stomach. She stood and followed her nose, hoping that Joe had tossed some eggs into the pan, as well. She stopped abruptly in the kitchen doorway.

"You're here?"

"Oui, c'est moi." *Yes, 'tis me.* Dickie poked a fork at the food sizzling in the pan. With a sideways glance, he said, "Did I give you a fright?"

"Of course not," she fibbed. "I knew you'd be back." Louisa walked towards him. "How did you get in?"

Rolling his eyes heavenwards, he said, "By the usual method." He inclined his head toward the back door.

"But I was keeping watch... I would have heard you."

"I was extra quiet. Even that so-called guard dog snoozed through."

"I can't believe I fell asleep," she groaned, annoyed with herself.

"Have you told him about our guests?"

Startled, she turned to face Joe. He was fully dressed and just about to light up a cigarette. She briefly appraised the rough blue canvas jacket and brown corduroys before letting her gaze fall to his bare feet. Oh, make that *almost* fully dressed.

"What guests?" Dickie asked sharply.

"Monsieur Dupont?" Alain poked his head round the door. "Would you, mm, like some more bread?" He proffered the large loaf in his hand.

"There's Pa, Ma and a bunch of kids." Louisa laughed at the bemused expression on Dickie's face. "Looks as though you'll be tied to that stove for a while yet." Before he could respond to her teasing, Louisa disappeared into the bedroom.

****

"The little Jewish family are kosher." Dickie, smirking at his own wit, greeted Louisa with a wave of his pipe. "Had a chat with them. He's a Gentile, the pater, so he can carry on as normal but his lady wife and kiddies will have to be moved to a safe house."

"Do you know of one?" Louisa asked.

Dickie nodded. "I have a reliable local who can find me anything we need. I'll get a message to him." He moved towards the front door, rapidly sucking on his pipe as if to send out smoke signals. "Keep an eye on them, will you?"

Louisa went out into the backyard. Joe and the three children had found a ball and were kicking it around. Judging by the laughter, they were having a good time.

Alain joined her to sit on the step. As they watched, Louisa basked in the feeling of the early morning sun on her face. Joe's bare feet didn't seem to be hampering him too much on the hard, rough cobblestones. But the dog, yapping excitedly, almost tripped him as it skittered backward and forward.

Joe gestured to the children. "Sshh."

Alain said to Louisa, "Ah, 'e doesn't need to worry. It's still early. The village is twenty minutes' walk away, so no one will 'ear. Nobody will 'ave noticed yet, mm, that we're not at 'ome." He checked his watch and frowned. "But I'll have to be back soon, to get ready to go to work. To act, mm, as if all is normal, you understand."

"Oui." Louisa gave Alain a sympathetic glance before returning her attention to the children. She noticed that they seemed to have grown too big for their clothes. The boy's jersey sleeves didn't even cover his wrists and both his sisters' pinafores were well above their knees. She laughed as Joe scooped up a giggling Mimi and swung her into the air in an effort to encourage her to release her firm grip on the ball. It worked. The dog seized the opportunity to pounce on it and was chased by the children around the yard.

"Have you both gone mad?" Dickie's sharp tone intruded on the happy scene. He glared, in turn, at both Joe and Louisa. Switching to French, he ordered, "Kiddies—get indoors and keep quiet."

Colette, her thin, pale face marked with deep shadows under her eyes, ushered the children into the living room. Louisa noticed that the woman had been forced to attach a yellow star denoting the status of Jew onto the lapel of her brown coat, and seethed with the injustice.

Dickie beckoned Louisa into the kitchen and shut the door. "Can you escort them to the contact? I have to stay for the next scheddy."

"When's the schedule due?" she queried.

"0900 hours."

Louisa knew the importance of these schedules. Dickie's role as radio operator was absolutely vital in maintaining communication with HQ. But then she remembered something that had been puzzling her. "By the way, where is the radio?"

"In a safe place," he replied enigmatically.

Louisa caught his tense expression. Reasoning that the radio operation was outside her responsibility, she decided against pursuing a detailed answer.

She began to pace the floor. "When will the car arrive?"

Dickie chuckled. "Dream on, Lulu. Petrol rationing, remember? I'm afraid it'll have to be horse and cart."

She stopped. "Oh no, are you saying that you expect me to drive a *horse?*"

"Listen, darling," he cajoled. "I know this kind of work isn't what you trained for but the chance to use

44

those skills will come. In the meantime, we must get the family out of here tout de suite." *Straight away.*

Louisa had to admit that he was correct. It was all hands to the deck. "All right. How hard can it be?"

"That's the spirit!" Dickie grinned approvingly as he moved towards the doorway. "I'll get stuck in with the arrangements."

Her peripheral vision caught the scrap of newspaper still lying where she'd left it the night before. She'd meant to question Dickie about that.

As Joe joined her, Louisa appraised him from top to bottom. "Dressed in that outfit, you look just like a peasant farmer."

Joe smiled. "Do I?"

She returned his smile. "I don't suppose you know anything about horses, by any chance?"

He raised both eyebrows. "Is Herr Hitler a Nazi? I often ride my horse back home on the farm."

"Then you're the man for me!"

Joe took a step back. "Whoa! Just what are you up to?"

She laughed and said, "Don't panic. You'll like this."

After her explanation, Joe said, "And what'll your mate Dickie say?"

"You just leave him to me." Louisa winked confidently.

****

Joe sat to haul on his damp socks. He didn't have time to wait for them to dry. Dickie had turned up with the horse and cart, borrowed from a neighboring farmer and Louisa had managed to persuade him to her way of thinking. There was still the vexing problem of shoes. Somehow he didn't think that his flying boots matched the peasant farmer look but there wasn't a likely alternative either.

At least, thanks to Alain, he now had a hat. The

45

Frenchman, when preparing to part from his tearful wife and family, had given it to Joe in gratitude for his help.

"Are you ready?" Louisa's soft voice set his heart racing. She stood before him, dressed in a skirt and clean white blouse, her hair brushed and shiny under a scarf, her lips adorned with fresh red lipstick, just begging to be kissed. He knew how soft, how sweet her lips were and felt a stirring of desire at the memory of their kiss the night before.

It must have been the moonlight, he thought. It had seemed easy to put aside the constant threat of danger and live for the moment.

His gaze lingered on her legs.

"Ghastly, aren't they?" she said, pulling a face. "Woollen stockings are so scratchy."

"They're not too bad," he said. "They match your underwear." He grinned as he stood to help her into her coat.

Recalling the incident in the kitchen, she blushed fiercely. "Ah... so you noticed?"

He bent his head towards her and murmured, "I noticed everything."

"Cheeky." She laughed, slapping his shoulder playfully.

A thrill of sensation pulsed through his body. As he caught her eye, she blushed again. Immediately, she bent to pick up her handbag and walked towards the bedroom, saying over her shoulder, "I think I'll take my little pillow." She patted her behind. "Might need some extra padding."

He thought, *don't worry, it's perfect just as it is...*

Whistling quietly, he strode outside and looked up at the sky. Not a cloud in sight. At least the weather was on their side. Maybe it was a good omen.

****

Louisa wriggled beside Joe as she adjusted to the rhythm of the swaying cart. She swiveled around to check that Colette and her three children were still well hidden behind piled-up sacks of potatoes. She wondered how they were bearing up. Dickie had tried to make it as comfortable as possible for the family, providing some sacking for them to lie on, but there was a limit to what could be done.

"Not far now," she commented, consulting the map which Dickie had sketched. She glanced at Joe. The rug draped over his legs to disguise his lack of footwear had slipped so she reached over and tucked it around him more firmly.

He was so polite, she thought after he'd thanked her, unlike *some* men she'd met. As she watched his confident handling of the horse, she was willing to concede that he was turning out to be much less of a hindrance than she had at first presumed.

They spent most of the journey in silence, allowing Louisa plenty of time to think. There were so many unanswered questions to put to Dickie, details he hadn't yet shared with her. There hadn't been time before, but as soon as they returned to the house, she'd tackle him.

"Look at that." Joe was pointing ahead at a figure clothed in black. It was the first person they'd seen.

"It's a nun," observed Louisa. She turned to the back. "Are you all right, Colette?" she inquired in French.

"Oui," was the muffled reply.

"Not long to go now."

As they drew alongside, the nun hailed them loudly.

Joe slowed the horse to a walk.

"Have mercy," the nun pleaded, puffing slightly in her effort to keep pace with them. "Help me to ze convent." She placed her hands together as if in prayer.

"Where is it?" asked Louisa, concerned.

She pointed down a side road. It was in the

opposite direction to where they were heading.

"Is it far?"

"Ah, oui." The nun blew her nose on the voluminous handkerchief she retrieved from her sleeve. "About forty minutes' walk." She sighed as she peered up at them with watery, pale blue eyes. "I fear my old bones won't make it."

Louisa glanced at Joe. The old woman looked exhausted but they really couldn't afford a delay. As if Joe could read her thoughts, he pointed to his watch.

She turned back to the distressed nun. "We are in a hurry...for the market." She indicated the sacks and shrugged. "I'm sorry, Sister, we can't help—" A tug on her sleeve interrupted her. "What is it, Joe?"

Joe's blank expression reminded her that she'd spoken in French. She couldn't blow their cover by reverting to English. Forced to disregard the likelihood of appearing rude, she leaned toward him to speak in his ear. "She wants a ride but it will mean a detour for us."

"We should help her. She can fit on the seat if we bunch up," he whispered back.

She shook her head. "We haven't got time. It's too risky."

The nun was taking off her shoes, wincing with the effort. Her large red feet were covered in blisters. She'd obviously walked a long way already.

"We have a half-hour in hand. We can't just leave her here—there's no one else to help."

Louisa sighed inwardly as Joe brought the horse to a halt. Extending her hand to the nun, she hauled her up and edged closer to Joe's strong, hard body.

Joe clicked his tongue and the horse sprang forward. The nun blew her nose again, said, "Merci," and "God bless" and plonked her plain, sensible black boots in her lap.

Louisa glanced at those shoes, and at the nun's feet, and an idea came to mind.

As the wheels crunched along the gravel towards the convent entrance, a muffled sneeze came from under the potatoes. Louisa glanced sharply at the nun, whose name she'd learned was Sister Benedict. She breathed a sigh of relief as she saw that the nun's face remained calm. Maybe she was a little deaf.

"Praise the Lord," exclaimed Sister Benedict, as a priest strode to greet her. "I'm not too late."

Sister Benedict invited them in for refreshments. Louisa declined but she insisted, assuring them that they still had plenty of time to get to the market. She said that she couldn't let them go without giving hospitality for their kindness.

Louisa swapped glances with Joe. How could she refuse without being rude and thus causing suspicion?

"Sister," she said. "We'd love to stay for a drink but we have an urgent appointment to keep. However, there is something you could do for us."

"What is that, my child?"

"Your shoes. Would it be possible...to give them to me?"

"Why would you want such uncomfortable old boots?" She quizzed Louisa with a glance, which turned into a frown when she noticed her feet. She clicked her tongue disapprovingly. "Far too big for you, anyway."

"They're not for me." Louisa thought quickly. "They're for... a friend. It's difficult to get larger sizes..." She glanced at Joe as her voice trailed off awkwardly.

Suddenly, the nun's face creased into a knowing smile. "Ah, oui!" And with a shrewd look, she added, "*Her* feet will be treated more kindly, I pray."

Louisa smiled gratefully. "Merci, you're most generous." She set them down on the seat next to Joe. "Au Revoir." *Goodbye.*

The contact, a scowling young man identified by the codename Vintage, grumbled that they'd made the rendezvous with only seconds to spare. Louisa let out a huge breath of relief as she handed over Colette and the children. With farewell hugs completed, she wished the family well. With any luck, the remainder of their trip would be relatively smooth sailing.

"These shoes fit very well," Joe remarked as he bent to tie the laces. "Fancy that old girl having feet the same size as mine."

"Luckily for you," Louisa said with a grin, "they bear little resemblance to any footwear that chic mademoiselles would want to be seen in. So, don't worry, I'm sure your masculinity is not at threat."

Joe laughed.

The horse moved forward, its hooves rhythmically clomping along the dusty road. The breeze flowed across Louisa's cheeks, lifting the hair around the edges of her scarf. She began to relax. Joe transferred the horse's reins to one hand and slid the other around her waist. A delicate tremble of excitement shimmied all the way down to her toes. She reached to squeeze his hand and caught his glance. "We made it. Well done, Joe."

They both lurched forward as a loud squealing from the left-side wheel brought the horse and cart to a jarring halt. At precisely the same moment, Louisa became aware that two men on bicycles were heading towards them.

"Quick, get into the field. Pretend you're answering nature's call."

As Joe leapt into the ditch, Louisa watched the men's rapid approach. Her mouth went dry as the gendarmes slowed down and stopped.

Chapter Five

"Bonjour Madame." One of the men dismounted and leaned his bike against the cart. "You are going to ze market?"

Louisa returned his greeting and, forcing a smile, indicated the sacks with a jerk of her thumb.

"Potatoes."

She watched his companion wheel his bike around to the back of the cart and begin inspecting the sacks.

"Ze day is beautiful, is it not?" the first man said. His expression seemed friendly. Her pulse rate slowed a little. There was no need to panic. She glanced at Joe. He was standing with his back towards them, apparently engrossed in his task.

She pretended to consult her wristwatch. "We have to get going." The friendly one nodded, took hold of his bike and began to walk towards his colleague.

"Joe!" she called.

Joe turned around and kicked the wheel nearest to him, dislodging a trapped stone. He stepped up beside Louisa. Touching his cap to the two men, he clicked his tongue in a command to the horse. As the cart began to roll forward, he said, "What did they want?"

Before she could answer, there was a shout from behind.

Louisa looked at Joe, her heart thumping wildly. Her own fear was reflected in the expression on his face.

The second policeman, the one who had been taking such an interest in the load, drew alongside.

Holding her breath, she braced herself for the demand to see their papers.

"How much, s'il vous plait?"

Louisa stared at the man in disbelief. "You want to buy a sack?"Acting quickly to cover Joe's look of confusion, she nudged him sharply with her elbow and pointed to the road ahead. To the policeman, she said, "Sorry, but they've all been pre-ordered."

The reins cracked across the horse's back. Rounding the corner, she burst into relieved laughter. That had been a close call. After all, she had no idea of the price of potatoes...

****

Dickie wasn't at the cottage when they returned. Louisa walked in, untied her scarf and tossed it, along with her pillow, onto the bed. She went into the lounge. A crumpled mauve cloth lay on the floor. She picked it up and then noticed that the table was missing. She looked around the room. Why would Dickie move it? She went into the kitchen and laid the cloth on the bench. A note was nearby. She picked it up and began to read.

"What's up?" Joe interrupted, striding in.

"Dickie's at a rendezvous." She flipped the paper over to examine the back. "That's all it says."

Joe located the cheese and bread and began to cut the loaf into thick slices. "Could he be making arrangements to get me back to England?"

"I don't know." Disappointed with the terse note, Louisa screwed it into a ball and heaved it at the bin.

Joe set out plates and pulled out her chair. Seating himself opposite, he gave her a measured glance. "Are you going to tell me what the matter is?"

She shrugged. "It's nothing."

From the wry expression on his face, she knew that he didn't believe her. He offered her some bread. "Let me guess. Dickie's keeping his cards close to his chest. And this is frustrating you to hell. Am I right?"

The perceptiveness of Joe's remarks unnerved her. She slapped a piece of cheese on the bread. "There just hasn't been time to have a proper meeting with him. If anything went wrong in the field, which in our case was the landing, then we were told to use our initiative. I suppose that's simply what Dickie is doing."

"How did you come to be separated from one another?"

"I was the first out of the plane. When I heard the gunfire, I presumed he hadn't made it." She shook her head in amazement. "I can't tell you what a relief it was to see him again."

"How would he have known about this house?"

"Personal contacts, probably. He has friends here."

Joe reached for the cider. "Fancy a drink?"

Louisa nodded, feeling a sudden glow of warmth at the secure feeling that his genial companionship gave her. It had only been a short time since they'd met, yet it was nice to know that she wasn't alone.

She allowed her gaze to settle on his lips. She imagined her finger tracing the full shapeliness of them and felt a tingle of desire, recalling the feather-soft touch as they had brushed across her own. She realized that, probably, she'd just been a momentary diversion for him. As for herself, he'd simply caught her at a vulnerable time. There were no emotional complications—it was merely a brief kiss.

Joe speared a piece of cheese with his knife. "How much do you really know about Dickie or of his activities?"

"I know he can be trusted. We trained together."

"Do you know where he got to last night?"

She sighed as she splayed her hands palm-down on the table. "I'm not his keeper, Joe. The reality is that we're dependent on him to operate the radio.

It's the only contact with our London Headquarters."

Joe shook his head. "I don't think it's fair of the man to keep you in the dark. When will you speak to him?"

"As soon as I can." Louisa shrugged. "But I'm sure he has everything under control." Their very survival depended on team loyalty. She got up from the table, trying to ignore her unease.

****

Louisa stretched to drape the dripping wet stockings over the line above the bath. She rolled the fineness of the silk between her fingers and grimaced anew at the thought of the woollen ones she was wearing. Before the war, she'd had dozens of silk stockings and luxurious underwear. Now she was reduced to just this one pair and plain, practical underwear such as her mother might own.

Harry would have laughed. He'd given her many gifts of beautiful lingerie, always wrapped in delicate layers of tissue paper. She could hear the rustle of that paper now, could almost feel the crinkle of it in her fingers.

Those were happy days—before the war. She squared her shoulders as if to push away a heavy burden and, at the same moment, felt Joe's arms steal around her waist and pull her back against him. She was startled momentarily, then, against her better judgement, folded her hands over his.

"I don't see you in the role of housewife," he murmured in her ear.

His rich tone sent an exquisite fluttering along her neck. She twisted around to face him. "The chores won't do themselves."

Her smile widened as Joe's gaze roamed over her face, seemingly absorbing every detail. She returned his glance with her own, delighting in the curve of his cheeks, the straight nose and the gleam of teeth in his wide, easy smile. Their eyes met and he quirked a questioning eyebrow.

"No, Joe," she breathed. "We can't—"

"But," he interrupted, "I find you irresistible."

Mon Dieu—he's good at this. It had been years since she'd allowed a man to seduce her. She'd successfully resisted others, so what was so different this time? A frisson of alarm edged into her mind.

She closed her eyes and as her traitorous body snuggled ever closer, she groaned aloud at her weakness. Joe's body instantly answered hers, his desire hardening against her stomach. Warm lips touched gently...teasingly light. He pressed a little harder, experimenting, exploring. Ripples of delight flowed through her. She returned his kiss, her hunger for him intensifying with each second. When their tongues met, he tasted of smoke-tinged, masculine heat, and fire seared her loins. Finally they paused for breath, and her eyes fluttered open to see him gazing at her with misty tenderness.

She flushed hotly, her heart beating a rapid tattoo against her ribs. She ought to stop this right now.

"We have the house to ourselves," he murmured. Again, he dipped his head toward her.

A key rattled in the lock of the cottage door.

They sprang apart with only a second to spare before they heard the thud of Dickie's boots in the hall. "Lulu? Are you back?"

Joe blew her a kiss, whispered, "Later," and was gone.

Louisa hurriedly closed the door and leaned against it, her legs shaking like jelly, her heart thumping. Reaching for the basin, she filled it and quickly splashed cold water over her face. She glanced into the mirror. Her tummy twisted at her reflection's silent accusation: how could she have been tempted to betray Harry's memory?

Gulping in deep breaths, she waited for her pulse rate to calm. As she reached for a towel, she heard the murmur of men's voices. There was an impatient rap-tap-tap on the door.

"I've brought someone to meet you, darling!" Dickie sounded jovial. "Chop, chop!"

"I'll be there in a second," Louisa called, patting her skin dry. With a final glance, she checked to be sure the telltale flush on her neck had disappeared.

Dickie loudly cleared his throat. "Delivery went okay? No problems?"

She opened the door and smiled a greeting. "It went very well, praise God."

"Jolly good!" Dickie beamed. "I also have good news."

She gave him a quizzical glance. "From HQ?"

He shook his head. "It's about Fisher." He twisted one end of his enormous moustache between two fingers. "He's moving on."

The words hit her like an unexpected slap. She knew she paled but fortunately Dickie didn't seem to notice.

She forced a weak smile.

"Yes." Dickie beamed with satisfaction. "Thought you'd be pleased to see him on his way." He placed a hand under her elbow and escorted her towards the living room. "Come and meet the fine chap who has arranged it all."

When Louisa saw who was standing by the fireplace, she stopped as if pulled up short on the end of a rope.

"Merde!" She put her hands on her hips. "What are *you* doing here?" The smirk on the man's face infuriated her. She glanced down and saw that he was wearing Joe's Air Force boots.

Dickie frowned, puzzled. "What's going on? Do you know Claude Frizon?"

"We meet again, Mademoiselle," Claude rasped, bending from the waist in a mock bow.

She scowled and turned to Dickie. "Why have you invited this swine into the house?"

"Louisa!" Dickie reproved. "Claude is our local

Maquis contact."

She stared at him. "He's *what*?" Louisa narrowed her eyes. "This oaf attacked me and then tried to make off with the Resistance funds."

Dickie, looking shocked, glanced sharply at Claude.

"Where's Joe? He'll confirm it." She raised her voice.

Claude sent Louisa a dark scowl. He kicked off the boots and headed for the door, muttering to Dickie, "I'll see you later."

As soon as he'd gone, Dickie demanded to know the whole story. Once she'd relayed it, he glowered in disbelief. "But he met me at the drop—it was through him that we have the use of this house."

"Whose house is it?" Joe asked, entering the room.

"It belongs to relatives of his. They're away for a month."

"Well, I don't trust him." Louisa pinched her bottom lip between her fingers. "Are you sure he's not a collaborator?"

"He can't be." Dickie shrugged off her concern. "He's not shown any sign of being a security risk. And besides, he's too useful to us. We don't have any choice but to trust him at the moment."

Louisa knew that it would be impossible to persuade Dickie merely by argument, even if her instincts told her she was right. She stared pensively at the cloth, which was back on top of the low table. Or was it a box? She lifted a corner of it.

Before she could say anything, Dickie said, "It's the radio set. I had to move it out to another house to make the scheduled broadcast. Claude warned me that a detector van was in this area."

"Oh." Louisa let the cloth fall back into place. "Well, that's one mystery solved. Any messages?"

Dickie glanced meaningfully at Joe. "Excuse us for a minute, old chap?"

Joe gave the thumbs-up sign to Louisa as he left.

She sat down. Dickie emptied his pipe into the fire grate and sat next to her. "There's a big operation coming up. An American, code named Ace, will make contact within the next day or so."

"What about Joe?" Her heart beat a little faster as she waited for Dickie's reply.

"Ace will be in touch about that, too."

"How long?"

Dickie pursed his lips. "Don't know. HQ couldn't verify. Could be anytime."

Louisa watched him fill his pipe with tobacco. As he struck the match to light it, she said, "Don't you think it's strange that out of that night's reception group, Claude Frizon was the only one to survive?"

Dickie's moustache wobbled like aircraft wings on take-off as he rapidly puffed out small clouds of smoke. "Not really," he said, talking out of the side of his mouth. "Could've been luck." He removed the pipe and pointed it toward her to emphasise his next point. "Anyway, darling, as I've said, we're dependent on him right now, whether you like it or not."

Louisa rose and paced the room. "There's another thing I wanted to ask you about, too."

"What's that?"

"I found a scrap of paper in the kitchen." She faced him squarely. "A German newspaper—can you explain that?"

Dickie was instantly on his feet. "Show me."

As they entered the kitchen they saw Joe dividing a rabbit into portions, the knife flashing in the late afternoon sunlight. He paused to look at them both, his eyebrows rising at the frown on Dickie's face.

Louisa noticed a large page of paper on the floor. She bent to pick it up and handed it to Dickie. "It was similar to this."

"The rabbit was wrapped in that," Joe said.

Dickie's eyes widened.

"What is it?" Louisa said, alarmed.

"He...Claude...brought us that bunny."

Louisa glanced at Joe. He arched an eyebrow before turning away to drop the pieces of meat into a pot.

"He'll need a good explanation for this," Louisa said.

"Darn right he will," Dickie affirmed.

****

Joe stood in the shelter of the porch, rolling a cigarette. Smoothing the white paper, he eagerly recalled the taste of Louisa's kisses. His fingers trembled as he opened the flat tin, pinched out a wad of tobacco, savored the familiar, acrid smell. He briefly closed his eyes, allowing the memory of Louisa's sweet scent to overtake him. Moistening the paper with his tongue, his imagination drove him to suppress a groan.

His nerve endings sizzled like the match he'd struck to life. He yearned to be close to her again, take her in his arms, feel her lips on his.

Searching the dusky sky as he heard the distant drone of planes returning to England, he wondered which of his fellow pilots had survived to fight another day.

Joe was well aware that passion flared quickly amidst grave uncertainty; risks were taken that mightn't occur in peace time. But he'd never met another girl quite like Louisa. She was special enough to take any amount of risk for. How could he ensure her safety?

He patted the dog, as it noisily scoffed its share of the rabbit stew, and silently made a promise to himself.

He would not leave France without her.

****

"Are you absolutely certain that you want to do

it?" Dickie dried the last dish and placed it on the shelf.

Louisa briskly wiped down the bench. "You want the truth? I hate the thought of having to be anywhere near that awful man." She dried her hands on Dickie's towel. "But it would give me a lot of satisfaction to catch him red-handed."

Dickie frowned. "What if he tries to assault you again?"

She smiled grimly. "I'll be ready for him this time."

"I'm not sure that it's such a good idea, darling."

"Let me try, s'il vous plaît."

Dickie, considering this, fidgeted nervously with the ends of his moustache. Finally, he said, "You'll have to be very careful." He put his hand on her shoulder and glanced at his watch. "He'll be here at twenty-two hundred hours."

****

Shuddering with distaste at the thought of shadowing Claude, Louisa repeatedly struck the side of her hand on the edge of the cold, stone bench. Then she walked into the bedroom, put on her coat and checked her handbag.

"I'll be back as soon as I can," she told Joe as he entered the room.

To her relief, he didn't press her for details. Instead, he drew her to him, cradled her face between his hands and kissed her, long and slow. Warmth radiated through her, building into deep, throbbing heat. She didn't want it to end but as her knees threatened to give way, she dragged her mouth from his and raggedly drew in some air.

Searching her face, he said, "I'll wait up for you."

She nodded. She could not bring herself to say goodbye.

Chapter Six

Louisa heard Dickie speaking quietly with Claude at the door. As soon as he'd gone, she strode out into the cool evening. Shivering, she buttoned up her coat.

Claude headed off towards the village. His footsteps made no sound on the soft grass verge edging the road. When he picked up pace, Louisa walked a little faster and she stumbled over a hidden tree root. At the twinge of pain, she swore under her breath.

As they neared the dim, grey shapes of the buildings ahead, she tried to anticipate where he was going. The only information Dickie had given her was that Claude had a lot of contacts in the village. Under her surveillance, she'd soon find out precisely who they were.

Abruptly, he stopped and looked furtively behind him.

She shrank against a stone wall. He glanced around again before turning into a narrow cobbled lane between shuttered houses. Louisa moved forward, noting the village streets seemed deserted. The occasional slit of light under a door was the only indication of occupants. She trod carefully on the paving, keeping her footsteps light and noiseless.

Ahead of her, Claude ducked down a side alley under the low-hanging sign of a café. Muted laughter and the low hum of patrons' voices spilled out from under the shutters.

She ran, catching up in time to see him knock on a door. Crouching behind an iron seat in the shadows, she watched as the door opened, sending a shaft of bright light across the cobbles. A man stepped out. It was Alain Pelet.

Louisa, covering her mouth in surprise, watched in puzzled amazement as the two men greeted each other. It didn't make any sense, but could Alain be a collaborator?

Claude handed him a packet. Alain partially unwrapped it, looked it over and sniffed it. He then gave Claude a thick wad of notes.

"Do you have more of that *Boche* paper?" Claude asked. "It makes good, strong wrapping."

"I'll gather it up after we've closed," Alain promised. "Can you get me some more of this Camembert? It's very popular with the officers."

Louisa smiled to herself. Now she understood. Alain's business was the café and obviously Claude was dealing food on the black market. Thus the mystery of the source of the German newspaper was solved but instinct warned her that her night wasn't over yet...

She waited until Claude had almost returned to the beginning of the alley before she crept out after him. A sharp wind had sprung up, stirring small piles of dusty leaves and rattling through the trees above.

Claude had made good use of his head start and was well in front of her, his jacket sides flapping open behind him. He hurried in the direction from which they had come but then suddenly disappeared around a corner.

Merde! She mustn't lose him. Louisa broke into a sprint, her breath coming in sharp bursts as she struggled against the pull of the wind. She turned the corner and saw him head into the entrance of a small hotel.

By the time she got there, he was already trudging up the narrow stairs. He must be meeting his contact in one of the rooms, she thought. Without hesitation, she followed him inside. When he stopped to knock at one of the doors, she hid behind a hall curtain. As he went in, she moved forward and cocked her ear to the door.

She shrank back as voices came from the direction of the staircase.

"Bonsoir!" *Good evening!* Two young women dressed in similar scarlet cocktail frocks sauntered toward her, smiling widely. "You must be Simone." Flanking her, they each took one of her arms and continued walking.

She tried to resist. "No, you are mistaken."

To her astonishment, they giggled, exchanging knowing looks with each other as one said, "Of course you are a leetle shy. Everyone is ze first time."

Louisa stopped, hastily freeing her arms from theirs. "What *are* you talking about?" She stared in disbelief from one to the other, noting the heavy makeup and the plunging necklines. As it began to dawn on her just what kind of establishment she had wandered into, there was a sound of thundering boots on the stairs.

The two women quickly vanished.

Louisa turned around to face two armed policemen. One of them restrained her. She watched as the other gendarme searched all the rooms, eventually extracting the two women, a man, and another girl.

There was no sign of Claude.

"What...whom...are you looking for?" Louisa boldly asked.

Ignoring her question, they hustled her and the rest of the group down the stairs and into two waiting vehicles.

Hemmed in between two of the females, Louisa wrinkled her nose at the stomach-churning smell of cheap perfume mingled with a sweat born of fear.

Merde! Where had Claude, that slippery bastard, disappeared to? And how was she going to get herself out of this situation?

One of her companions began to sob, wrapping her thin arms around herself and huddling, shivering, against Louisa. With a sense of disgust, Louisa realized that the girl was little more than a child.

Louisa unbuttoned her coat and spread as much of it as she could across the girl's trembling knees. She was rewarded with a glimmer of a smile.

Arriving at the local gendarmerie they were all briskly bundled into cells. Louisa looked around in despair at the grey walls, the bucket in the corner, the bare bunk beds and the one small, high window. She gagged at the stench of stale urine. A hollow opened in her stomach as a shudder of revulsion swept through her. Tears stung her eyes and she bit hard on her bottom lip.

A guard beckoned to Louisa, then unlocked the door. In the split second that his attention was diverted, she shoved her revolver under the mattress. It wouldn't be wise to be caught in possession of a weapon. The guard escorted her to a small room, leaving her there with another larger, uglier gendarme, who ordered her to sit on the chair in front of him. Then he demanded her handbag.

Louisa, her mouth dry, watched in trepidation as he riffled through the contents. He fired a barrage of questions at her, lifting each item, assessing its worth. Then he demanded, "Why were you out during curfew?"

Louisa was prepared for this. Holding his gaze, she answered, "Caring for my friend...she has been very ill with suspected polio."

At the mention of the infectious disease, the gendarme visibly recoiled. But then a skeptical look passed over his face. He pulled out a fistful of francs and waved them under her nose. "Zis money—where did you get it? You are a prostitute, oui?"

"M'sieur!" she protested. "Non!"

He fixed her with a steely glare and roared, "Ze only people who carry around this much money are prostitutes or members of ze Maquis!" He repeated the first question, this time accompanying it with a stinging slap across her face.

Louisa's head snapped back. She clenched her fists by her sides as red hot anger burned in her chest. Determined not to be intimidated by his bullying, she searched for a reasonable explanation for the money, but before she could think of one, she was interrupted by the door opening.

Another gendarme stepped into the room. Instantly, she recognized him as the one who had wanted to purchase the potatoes. By the curl of his mouth, she knew he'd also recognized her. Her heart raced. Could this make her predicament even worse?

He walked over to her, indicating the money in the interrogator's hand. "I see zat you made a good profit from your potatoes, Madame."

She stared, momentarily stunned at this turn of events. Recovering quickly, she nodded hard as if in agreement and flashed him a grateful smile.

The bully scowled and studied her identity card. "Madame? You have a husband?" He shot her a hard look. "It says here zat you are a Mademoiselle!"

He gestured towards the door. "Lock her up for ze night." A sneer distorted his lips. "We'll see if anyone comes to claim her."

"Who are they looking for?" she quietly asked her escort as soon as they were out of earshot.

"Saboteurs." He bent his head towards her. "Zey've heard zat ze Resistance are planning somezing big, so zey've ordered a crackdown."

Louisa was instantly alert. It must be the operation which Dickie had briefed her about.

As she heard the key grating in the lock behind her, she balled her hands into fists. Claude was behind this. She was sure of it. It would certainly explain how he'd managed to elude the round-up.

Her stomach tightened into knots as she fought down her frustration. If only she'd been able to catch him out sooner.

She stretched out wearily on a bunk. How was she going to get out of this?

Throughout the long night, Louisa tossed and turned on the lumpy, rank mattress. She thought of Joe waiting and watching back at the cottage. If only there was a way of getting word to him. Her body warmed at the memory of his kisses as she slipped into oblivion.

As soon as it was light, she sat up and stretched her legs. She could hear no sound from any of the other cells. Everyone must still be asleep.

The friendly gendarme came into view.

"When will they let me go?" she asked him.

"I cannot say, Mademoiselle." He gave her a sympathetic look. "You are ze only one here. Ze others were released last night."

Turning away from him, she sank down slowly onto the bunk, staring blankly at the wall as she absorbed the fact that she was alone. Totally alone. How would Dickie know where she was? Even if he did know, he would be powerless to help her. It was too risky. A sudden surge of panic gripped her. Was this the end to her freedom?

"Come." She heard the gendarme unlocking the cell door. Quickly, before he glanced up from his task, she retrieved the hidden revolver and shoved it safely into her coat pocket.

Louisa stumbled clumsily, reluctant to face another interrogation. She drew in shallow gasps of breath as perspiration prickled along her spine. She found herself being escorted to the front desk, where a man stood beside another guard.

The man turned around to face her. It was Claude, a grin of recognition appearing on his face—the idiot! She ignored him, carefully keeping her face expressionless. He'd obviously been apprehended as well and it would do neither of them any good to show that they knew each other.

She glanced at the entrance door. Could she make a run for it?

Claude took a step toward her, still grinning widely, as if to indicate this was all a huge joke. The pair of gendarmes were also smiling. Suddenly, she realized that they were not detaining Claude at all. They were treating him as a free citizen.

Before she could react, he made to kiss her on both cheeks and whispered in her ear, "Do try to look at least a little fond of me. I've told zem zat you're my mistress." He slipped his arm into hers, saying loudly, "We'll soon be home, *chérie...*"

"How on earth did you get away with it?" Louisa asked as soon as they were outside, looking nervously back over her shoulder. Any moment now, she was sure that a shout would call them back.

She hurried alongside Claude, lifting her face to allow the drizzly rain to refresh her hot skin. It was galling that Claude, of all people, had been the one to get her out of that place.

Claude wiped the back of his hand across his nose and handed her a piece of paper. "Zis convinced zem."

Louisa scanned it quickly and gasped out loud. "You're a member of the Milice?"

His lip curled in a sneer. "It's fake, of course."

Louisa didn't know whether to believe that or not. But if he really was a member of the civilian force, then why would he have bothered to rescue her? And then, as another thought struck, she asked carefully, "How did you know that I'd been arrested?"

She watched his face as a smirk played across his lips. "Fortunately for you," he leaned closer to her in a conspiratorial manner, "*Simone...*" His eyes narrowed. "I heard you wiz ze girls."

"What were you doing there?"

"Never you mind." He tapped his nose. "It is private business."

It was obvious he was a womanizer, she thought. Unless there was another reason he'd been there...something to do with the Resistance?

"Don't deny zat you were following me," he growled.

Louisa stayed silent until they reached the cottage. How would Dickie react? The knowledge that she'd failed to incriminate Claude was bad, but even worse was the fact that she was now in his debt. Someday, somewhere, he would expect repayment. A shiver ran down her spine.

He left her at the door, slinking away into the mist like some feral animal trying to hide. No doubt he didn't want to face any awkward questions from Dickie. She knocked and, while waiting to be let in, imagined Joe's welcoming smile.

No one came to the door. Were they still in their beds? She knocked a little louder and, at the same time, noticed that the dog's collar and chain lay abandoned on the ground. The animal was probably out back. Sidestepping to the window, she tried to peer through but the curtains were tightly drawn.

She twisted the door handle and, to her surprise, the door swung inwards. Strange that Dickie hadn't locked it. She closed it behind her and walked through to the kitchen. The rich, lingering smell of last night's stew made her stomach clench hungrily. First things first, she decided. She was back safe and sound. No need to disturb the boys' beauty sleep just yet. She opened the curtains, slipped off her handbag and coat and set about finding some sustenance.

Half an hour later, after she'd done her best to cleanse herself of the stench and grime of the night, it began to dawn on her just how quiet the cottage was. No sounds of snoring or movement, no dog noises from the yard. An eerie feeling crept up the back of her neck. She cautiously negotiated the hallway, stood clear and pushed open the main bedroom's door.

"Joe?" she called tentatively. She listened for a response. "Dickie?" No reply.

She looked toward the bed and could see that it was occupied. Tiptoeing closer, her heartbeat quickened.

His head was tucked down into the sheets. Holding her breath, she shook his shoulder. She jumped as the figure suddenly stretched out an arm, brushing against her leg.

"Joe?" Opening one bleary eye, Joe groaned and struggled to a sitting position. He stretched out his arms and yawned loudly.

"Mon Dieu!" Louisa wrinkled her nose at the sickly-sweet smell of cider. "So much for waiting up for me! You and Dickie made a night of it, did you?"

"Now, hang on a minute." Joe shot her an aggrieved look. "We waited up for you for hours! But when you hadn't returned by midnight, we—"

"Showed your concern by drinking yourselves under the table?"

"Give me a break," he groaned. He put his hands on her upper arms and drew her closer. "What happened? Where have you been?"

"I was caught in a Gestapo round-up." Louisa grimaced. "And ended up spending the night in a stinking police cell."

Joe's eyes widened. *"You what?"* He seized her hands and stroked them as she filled him in on the events thus far. When she'd finished, his gaze searched her face. "Are you all right?"

She attempted a shaky smile, hoping to convince him she was fine.

"Thank God," he whispered. He held her gaze for a long moment before attempting to rise from the bed. Pulling a face, he complained, "I'm as crook as a dog." Noticing her puzzled glance, he explained,

"That is…I feel…sick." He clutched his stomach.

Louisa helped him up before easing her hands out of his grasp. "Where's Dickie?"

Joe raised an eyebrow. "Isn't he back? He went out to find you."

Louisa gasped. "*Merde!*"

"It may not be that bad," Joe reassured her as he reached for his shoes. "He's spent a night out before, remember."

Louisa frowned. "But this time he could be in real danger!" She turned on her heel and strode to the doorway, her head spinning with possible scenarios of what might have happened to him.

Joe followed her into the living room. "What do you mean?" He reached out and swung her round to face him. "What is it you know?"

Louisa hesitated. How much should she reveal to him?

"Tell me," Joe prompted. "Perhaps I can help."

"All right," she finally agreed. "The Milice—the local militia—have discovered highly sensitive information about the Resistance. I don't know how much they know…they seem to be arresting people at random. If Dickie's found in the wrong place at the wrong time…" She broke off as she recalled the pain of the brute's hand connecting with her cheek. Her fingers sought out the tender place.

Noticing her movement, Joe bent forward to ease her hand gently away and pushed back her hair. "You have a nasty bruise there." He looked into her eyes, his lips compressed. "Is Frizon behind this?"

Louisa's throat tightened as the horrors of the night loomed before her—that ghastly little cell and the dread of the interrogator's abuse. She sank her head onto Joe's shoulder, taking advantage of his reassuring masculinity. "It will be far worse for Dickie if he's caught."

Joe's hands slipped down her arms to her wrists.

"I have a confession to make. He told me what you were up to last night. And..." Joe cleared his throat, "I said that he was being bloody irresponsible sending you out like that."

"He didn't make me do it. I *wanted* to."

"All the same, he shouldn't have even asked you. He could have done the job himself."

"You know nothing about it, Joe."

"I've seen what Claude is capable of."

Louisa, though flattered by his concern, threw her hands in the air in frustration. "You must let me do my job!"

"But do you have to fight the whole darned war entirely by yourself?"

"Now you're being ridiculous."

"Am I?" His lips twisted cynically. "I just don't see why you need to take on unnecessary risks."

"Calculated risks," she corrected. "Don't you do the very same thing each time you fly over enemy territory?"

He shook his head. "But you're so vulnerable."

"Because I'm a woman? Don't be so naïve."

His gentlemanly, protective chivalry was charming but totally inappropriate—at least in this century. Had he, in spite of her efforts, still not caught up to the fact that she played an equal role to any man in this war?

She eyed him challengingly. "You have no respect for me at all, do you!"

An obstinate glint appeared in his eye. "That's not true...I just don't trust Claude Frizon." He caught her hand. "Promise me that you'll keep away from him."

If only it were that simple. "I'll try."

But even as the words left her lips, she decided that the sooner Joe left for England, the better. He was plainly starting to care for her and that was the last thing she wanted right now. She refused to admit, even to herself, that just maybe she was

71

developing feelings for *him*.

Pulling away, she said, "Get your kit together, Joe. If Dickie hasn't returned by noon, we'll evacuate to a safer billet."

****

Louisa had just gathered up her dry washing from the bathroom and stuffed it into her kitbag when she heard a series of knocks on the back door.

She hurried over. "Who is it?"

"Ace." A pause. "At your service, ma'am."

The American accent was clear. Texan, if she wasn't mistaken. This had to be the contact Dickie had mentioned.

One further check. "Why are you here?"

"I've a package to collect."

The 'package' would be Joe. Dickie had said that Ace would arrange to move Joe along. She opened the door. A tall, thin, auburn haired man, dressed like a partisan in brown trousers, shirt and jacket, stepped quickly inside and tipped his cap to her.

"Morning, ma'am," he drawled. Water dripped from the cap onto the floor. "Is Dickie here?"

"Afraid not," Louisa answered. "Last night I was picked up for questioning." She ushered him into the kitchen and shut the door. "Dickie went out and we haven't seen him since."

Ace looked alarmed. "How much do they know?"

"They seem to be informed of the planned operation but not the details."

"What did ya tell them?"

"Nothing." Louisa shrugged, adding meaningfully, "I don't know anything."

Ace lowered his long limbs onto a chair and sat, crossing his legs at the ankles. His brow was furrowed in thought. "Change of plan. I'll stay here in case Dickie makes contact." He glanced at her. "Can ya take the airman to the station? He'll be met there and escorted onto the train." He glanced at his watch. "There's an automobile outside. It should get y'all there by 0930 hours."

A car? "Are you certain?" She'd ceased to believe in such luxuries.

"Sure. If you leave now y'all get there right on time. I've even arranged a driver for ya."

"You Yanks are unbelievable!" she said, her voice full of admiration. She left the room to tell Joe.

****

Joe put down the razor and scooped water from the basin onto his face. Leaning towards the mirror, he stroked the line of his jaw. It'll do, he thought. As he gathered up and pocketed his few essential possessions, Louisa stole into his mind. He could easily understand her wanting to be involved in a cause which she believed in. He could almost accept her needing to contribute as an equal to men.

What he couldn't quite get his head around was why she had no qualms about putting herself in danger. It was as though she didn't care about the consequences. Why would she do that?

Hearing footsteps in the hall, he turned to watch her enter the room. He marvelled that, apart from the bruise, she showed no ill-effects from her grim experience. She was still heart-wrenchingly lovely. After spending half the night thinking about her, worrying about her, aching for her, she'd even followed him into his dreams.

His stomach knotted in angst at their approaching separation. A reminder of the promise he'd made to himself, to not leave the country without her, crossed his mind.

But as to the way to achieve it, he had no idea. His heart sank at the realization that he was competing with her zealous dedication to the partisan cause. And he admired her for that, even if she didn't realize it...yet. The only guide he had to her feelings about him was the way she'd responded to his advances. His hunch was that deep passion simmered just under the surface...they just needed to give it more time.

There was no time. With a heavy sigh of frustration, he acknowledged that if he were a betting man, he'd have to say that the odds were heavily stacked against him.

****

After completing her preparations to leave, Louisa led Joe into the kitchen to meet the visitor.

"Thanks, mate," Joe said to the American as they shook hands.

"Bonne chance!" *Good luck!* Ace called after them as they splashed through the shallow puddles to the idling black Renault. Its exhaust belched out thick clouds of choking black smoke.

"Running on charcoal," Joe observed, coughing, as he opened the back door for Louisa.

Gunning the accelerator, the driver sent the car slithering across the muddy yard and onto the road. His head was almost completely covered with a navy blue beret but even so, there was something about his neck which aroused Louisa's curiosity.

She leaned forward, caught his eye in the rear vision mirror and gasped. "Claude!"

Joe gave her a sharp glance. "What the blazes is he doing here?"

Claude put up his hand in a conciliatory manner. "I'm just following orders."

Joe fell silent but if looks could kill, Louisa thought, Claude's head would no longer be attached to his neck. Her mouth set in a grim line at the knowledge that, once again, she was dependent on Claude's assistance.

The car lurched. Joe gathered her to him, burying his face in her hair. His arms locked around her, as if he loathed to release her. The scent of tobacco lingered on his rough cotton shirt.

He whispered urgently, "Come with me..." but that was all Louisa heard as the car skidded to a squealing halt.

Chapter Seven

"We're here," Claude announced brusquely.

Louisa glanced out. The station building was still some way ahead. "It's still raining. Can't you get closer?" she asked.

Ignoring her, Claude gave a brisk nod to Joe. "Get out. You'll be met here."

Joe hesitated, his grip tightening around Louisa as she tried to ease herself away.

"Go on, Joe, you're on your way home," she urged. She grasped his hands, giving them a squeeze. "It's what you wanted, isn't it?"

"Hurry up," Claude growled, wrenching open Joe's door. "Your escort has arrived."

As she met Joe's gaze, her heart tugged at the anguish in his eyes. His lips curved bravely as she leaned forward and kissed him on the cheek. She rubbed at the red lipstick smudge with her thumb and whispered, "Godspeed."

Claude leaned forward into the car. With an impatient gesture, he yanked out a coat stored under Joe's legs. A train whistle sounded in the distance.

Joe swore under his breath, glowering darkly at Claude.

"I'll be fine," Louisa reassured briskly. "My work is here. Dear Joe, take this opportunity." She hugged him again. "You *must* go."

As she watched him stride away with his companion, the soft, drizzly rain drifted like a damp shawl across her shoulders. A lump rose in her throat as, without looking back, he raised one hand in a silent, poignant farewell.

She turned back to the car, fighting down her

feelings. But her efforts were instantly sabotaged as a brutal shaft of pure pleasure hit her between the thighs in a cruel reminder of his kisses and his soulful eyes. Clenching her muscles against this torture, she forced herself to face facts. There had never been the possibility of a future with Joe. Besides, she reminded herself, now that he was safely on his way, she could fully focus on her task.

She sighed. The plain reality was that if Joe had known of all the future risks she faced, he'd only have tried to stop her. And *that* would have compromised all her plans.

****

Joe set one foot in front of the other, mechanically keeping pace with the loping gait of his escort, introduced to him as M'sieur Michel. His morose companion kept his head down against the rain. Apart from an initial greeting, the chap had not spoken two words. That suited Joe. It gave him a chance to dwell on Louisa.

He'd only known her for a few days but that didn't matter—he knew what he felt. His personal danger paled into insignificance at the thought of any harm coming to her. The worst of it was that he'd soon be on his way to relative safety and his body ached to take her with him. If anything happened to her he'd never even hear about it—he'd been forced to leave her behind, in a world which was now closed off to him. It was a slim hope that he'd find her after the war—assuming the war would ever end...

Forcing his attention back to his silent companion, Joe realized that his safety was now in this man's hands. So many courageous people were willing to take the chance to play their part in sabotaging the enemy. Joe felt humbled and knew that he should be grateful.

An image of his parents came into his head. He recalled something his mother had said one day when he was about ten, as she paused briefly between the relentless round of farmhouse chores. "I should be getting on with the baking..." She'd gazed out the window at the brilliant blue, cloudless sky as she'd said it.

Just then, his father had come into the room. "Blow that!" he'd declared in his typically blustery manner. "The world's full of shoulds. Should do this, should do that... it makes a rod for your back, if you're not careful." He'd draped a beefy arm around her shoulders and given her a squeeze. "It's a corker day out there, Enid. Why don't we take a few sandwiches up to the lake and make the most of it?"

Joe could still remember the pang of disappointment he'd felt when his mother had insisted that she get on with her duties. They could all go on a picnic tomorrow, she'd said.

'Tomorrow' had dawned cloudy and cold, and rain had fallen steadily for three days after that...

Joe stepped onto the platform. Out of the corner of his eye, he noticed a small flash of black streaking past. He stopped and turned around to see the mongrel from the cottage, tail drooping and ears hanging flat, trotting in the direction in which they had just come. How did it get here?

Joe moved forward as his companion urged him on. Ahead of them, people gathered as the train, feisty steam spewing around its wheels, hissed to a stop. The doors clanged open and passengers trickled out.

Suddenly Joe realized that he was being spoken to—M'sieur Michel was earnestly trying to engage him in some sort of conversation—but as it was all in French, Joe could only understand a fraction of it. He just nodded and smiled occasionally and tried to look interested. It seemed to be the right thing to do as he was rewarded with answering smiles and nods. As soon as the man had handed him a ticket and forged identity card, the conversation and smiles abruptly ended and Joe turned around to find him gone. With a sigh of resignation, he squared his shoulders and boarded a carriage.

Just as he was about to sit down, Joe glanced through the window. What he saw made his heart suddenly race. What the dickens was the blighter playing at? Straightening up, he became aware of a commotion on the platform. People were milling around in an agitated fashion and then he realized why—a group of German guards was marching towards the train. They entered the next carriage and he could see people around him getting out their papers and identity cards.

Joe fished around in his pockets for the card he'd been given. His face burned as he failed to find it. Frantic, he searched again. He was sure that he'd slipped it into his jacket pocket. As the guards edged closer, he made a split second decision.

****

Louisa was about to step into the waiting car when suddenly she noticed the dog. It shot past her and stopped at the driver's side front wheel, cocking its leg against the tire. Claude immediately leaped out and aimed an enraged kick and a curse at the animal. The dog emitted a surprised yelp, and then slunk around to Louisa's side. She opened the back door for the dog to jump in.

"What are you doing?" Claude reached in and grabbed the dog by the scruff of its neck. The animal growled, backing into the corner.

"It's from the cottage!"

"The mongrel's not messing on my seats. It can find its own way home." Hauling the dog out, he dragged it towards a thick macrocarpa hedge.

Louisa slammed the door and ran after him. It occurred to her that Dickie may have taken the dog out with him. Maybe it could lead them to where he was.

"Wait!" she called.

Guided by the animal's growls of protest, she found Claude sheltering from the drizzle under the branches of a large beech tree. But the dog was nowhere in sight.

Between breaths, she said, "Where's it gone?"

"Forget it." Claude eyed her handbag. "Any cigarettes in zere?"

"But it may be able to help us find..." Realizing it was too late, her words trailed off. She hoped the dog could find its way home. She heard a click of cold steel. Claude was holding a knife.

"Give zat to me." He gestured to the handbag.

Louisa smiled grimly. "Are you that desperate for ciggies... or is it really my lipstick you're after?"

Claude wasn't amused. Adopting a threatening stance, he hissed through clenched teeth, "Hand me ze francs."

Louisa's eyes narrowed. He had risked getting her out of custody and was now attempting to call in his debt, just as she'd suspected he would. Stubbornly determined not to give in to his demand, she said firmly, "Dickie will—"

"He's dead."

As the full impact of Claude's stark words sank in, a giant hole opened in the pit of her stomach. *Dickie's dead?* How could that be? What sort of trouble had he run into last night?

She stared at the knife in Claude's hand. A chill ran down her back as another thought struck—was Claude his killer? But why would he murder their only radio operator?

In the distance, a shrill whistle was followed by the sound of the train moving off. *Joe is safely on his way.*

A man's shout distracted Claude. As he half-turned to see who it was, Louisa lunged, shoving him hard enough to knock him off-balance.

He staggered a few steps back. Righting himself almost immediately, he spun around with a roar of rage.

She ducked to the side, feeling for her revolver while eyeing the knife blade.

He raised it.

As the knife came down, she twisted away. The blade narrowly missed her, slashing instead across a knobbly tree root. Before she could recover, the dog suddenly leapt between them.

"Get in behind!" The sharp command startled them both.

The dog spun around, barking furiously and advanced menacingly towards Claude.

Louisa watched in astonishment as the dog forced its target back towards the tree trunk. Baring its teeth, it leapt towards him. Claude gave an anguished shout.

A man appeared, forcing Louisa to redirect her aim.

"Hey, don't shoot." It was Joe. He turned to the dog. "Leave!" he yelled.

But before the dog could obey, Claude plunged his knife into the dog's neck and the animal dropped, lifeless, to the ground. With his free arm, Claude lashed out and knocked the gun from Louisa's hand. Picking it up, he fixed Joe with a menacing glare. "Keep out of zis."

Claude motioned to Louisa to come closer. Throwing Joe a quick warning glance, she did as she was told.

"You owe me, mistress," Claude jeered. "You'd still be rotting in zat cell if I hadn't saved you."

Joe drew in an audible breath.

Claude aimed the gun at Joe's head. "Don't move."

Louisa swung the handbag into Claude's face, screaming, "Here, take the goddamn money!"

He staggered. Joe grabbed him and forced him into a headlock.

Louisa raised a hand and dealt Claude a precise

blow on his thick neck. Joe released his grip and the heavy, limp body slumped forward.

****

"Thank our lucky stars that the big fool left the key in the ignition." Louisa jammed the car into gear, not daring to look back. As they bumped along the road, she stole a quick glance at Joe. He seemed as calm as if they were merely out for a Sunday drive. How could he be so composed? Louisa's hands began to shake. She gripped the wheel more firmly. She'd find out later why he'd taken it into his head to miss out on his chance for freedom.

But for now, all she could think of was Dickie. How had the poor sod died? Grief, mixed with the fear that just now Joe had only narrowly missed the same fate, boiled up like white heat inside her. She bit out, "You could have been killed back there!"

Joe's jaw hardened. "So could've you."

They coasted to a stop outside the cottage. It had stopped raining.

Ace strode out to greet them. He frowned when he saw Joe. "Something go wrong, buddy?" He turned to Louisa. "Where's Claude?"

Joe cleared his throat. "There was a last minute change of plan."

Louisa raised her eyebrows at Joe and tossed the car keys to Ace. "We'll talk inside."

As Ace parked the car in the barn, Louisa rounded on Joe. "You should be halfway home by now—what got into you?"

Joe grinned. "Should? Blow *should!*" He grabbed her hand and pulled her into the dwelling. He pressed her against the wall, placed his hands on either side of her waist and met her eyes. "Aren't you just a little pleased that I came back to find you?"

Tension welled up inside her. Captured under his passionate gaze, she could feel herself melting. His eyelashes flickered and he lowered his lips to hers, but she came to her senses and blocked the kiss with one hand. "Joe..."

He nibbled at her ear. "Mmm...?"

"Why did you come back?"

"You know why."

"That doesn't excuse the fact that you've just thrown our help back in our faces."

"Is that what you think?" he asked coolly.

"Sacrifices have been made..." Words failed her at the reminder of Dickie's fate. Twisting out of Joe's grasp, she moved away.

Joe misunderstood her. "It's a shame about the dog. He had potential."

"What?" Louisa, perplexed, furrowed her brow.

"As a sheepdog. I've trained a few back home."

"Oh...right." Louisa, who'd intended to tell him about Dickie, found herself murmuring, "Poor creature, it didn't deserve its fate." Nor Dickie, she thought, repugnance for the man's killer welling up inside her.

Ace came in. He said, "Claude was supposed to stay with y'all. What the hell happened?"

Louisa and Joe swapped glances. Had she dealt Claude a fatal blow or would he recover consciousness? It was clear that the only reason he'd rescued her from the gendarmerie was to get his hands on the money. He wouldn't have known, however, that included in her earlier preparations to leave had been the task of emptying her handbag of the francs and stashing them in a place she knew Dickie would discover. But now she'd have to rethink what to do. Louisa hesitated. How much should she tell Ace?

"We had a bit of a disagreement," she said.

"About him?" Ace indicated Joe.

"No." Louisa shook her head. "I..." She swallowed the lump in her throat. "I know what happened to Dickie. I think Claude killed him."

"He's dead?" Ace's eyes widened. "No, ya must be mistaken."

"But—"

"Dickie swung by while you folks were out. Didn't stay real long. Said he'd some kind of date—"

"That's right!" Joe corroborated. "I saw Dickie with a girl at the station."

"A woman? Are you sure?" Louisa stared at Joe. That didn't sound like the Dickie she knew.

"Petite...blonde...buxom?" Ace suggested.

"That's the one." Joe grinned. "They exchanged newspapers as she got off the train."

"Newspapers or phone numbers?" Ace quipped.

Joe laughed. "Well, at least we know that the old devil is alive and kicking, eh!"

Louisa sucked in her lip. It seemed as though Dickie was still up to his old tricks—playing the maverick and not letting everyone in on the plans.

She stole a glance at Joe. His observation of the newspaper exchange was sharp. As he and Ace turned towards the kitchen, she followed them, still deep in thought. One thing about this was not a mystery: from Joe's description, she knew exactly who the woman could be. But what was she up to and how much was Dickie involved?

She said nothing to Ace or Joe. There was no point. At least, not at this stage.

Louisa reached for the kettle. A ghastly idea edged into her mind—had Dickie told Monique that she was here? No, surely he'd have more sense than that. Dickie had heard her accuse Monique of treachery. He'd been the one to restrain her from trying to scratch the bitch's eyes out. He knew that she hadn't believed a word of Monique's protests of innocence.

****

Louisa stared absentmindedly at Ace over the rim of her cup. Joe had gulped down his tea and made himself scarce. She tried to concentrate on what Ace was saying, but her thoughts were miles away.

"Pardon me, ma'am," prompted Ace. "Did you get all—"

"Sorry," Louisa interrupted, lowering her cup and making an effort to give Ace her full attention. "You said something about the operation being postponed?"

"Until further orders," he drawled. "As I said, we think there's a weak link somewhere, with someone tipping off the enemy. Y'all can remain here for now, but Dickie will need to move to avoid radio detection."

She nodded, absorbing the fact that, obviously, Dickie had not informed him of their suspicions of Claude. "What about Joe?"

"He's your responsibility till another chance comes up." Ace shrugged. "He's one crazy fella missing an opportunity to get back to his squadron. Can't think what got into him."

An uncomfortable warmth infused Louisa's face. She knew that she was the reason for Joe compromising his chance. And even though she hadn't meant that to happen, she couldn't stop a pang of guilt. *Damn. Joe should've just stuck to the plan.*

If Ace noticed her blush, he was too polite to mention it, bless him. He merely checked his watch and stood up, saying, "Okay, I gotta go. If Claude turns up, tell him to report to me, will ya?" He reached down to pat Louisa's arm. "Don't you worry your pretty head, little lady. The frog may be a wily son-of-a-bitch but he's not a murderer. He knows this area like I know every hair on my horse's head and that kind of local knowledge is darned valuable to us." He smiled and gave her another reassuring pat. "He'll find his way back safely."

Louisa frowned. She didn't want to contemplate the possibility of seeing that vile oaf ever again. As soon as Ace had driven off, she went to the radio set and pulled out the hidden bundle of francs. It was all there. Counting out as much as she calculated she'd need, she replaced the balance and stood up just as Joe came into the room. He gave her a rueful glance as, seating herself on a chair, she gestured to him to do the same.

"I'm sorry if I got you into trouble," he said, drawing his tobacco pouch out of his shirt pocket.

She watched him roll a cigarette. When he'd lit up and taken his first drag, she said quietly, "No, I'm the one who should apologize—for giving you a hard time." At his raised eyebrow, she lifted one shoulder. "Claude was more dangerous than I'd imagined."

Joe blew out a stream of smoke and said with a grin, "You do seem to get yourself into some scrapes...don't you!"

Louisa rolled her eyes but refused to rise to the bait. Settling herself more comfortably and crossing her legs, she asked, "Can I trust you, Joe?" She thought she already knew the answer but she still searched his face. His candid gaze met hers, darkened with a look of...of...

"No," he murmured, "maybe you can't."

She flicked her tongue over suddenly dry lips. Heat pooled inside her as his eyes followed the move before recapturing her gaze once more.

"Er...I mean...with a secret," she hastily clarified, desperately fighting the desire to lean towards him.

"Oh." He lowered his eyelids. *"That* kind of trust." He stubbed out his cigarette and folded one leg over the other. "As they say on the posters in Britain, 'mum's the word.'" He mimed the sealing of his lips as if with a zipper.

She laughed, drew in a deep breath and began to inform him of her very personal reason for returning to France.

Chapter Eight

"From your description, I'm certain that the woman you saw at the station with Dickie is his ex-wife, Monique."

Joe pursed his lips in a low whistle. "Ex-wife, eh? I wouldn't have picked that. In fact, I had a feeling he was of another persuasion..." He waggled his eyebrows in comical fashion. "If you know what I mean."

Louisa chuckled softly. "It's true that they were never a conventional couple." She shrugged. "It was no secret that they both took other lovers. Monique was a social butterfly, society hostess, everyone's friend." Bitterly, she added, "It was only when this damned war started that her mask crumbled, exposing it for the superficial sham that it was."

Joe lolled back in his chair, hands behind his head and asked, "You knew her well?"

"Her papa owned a newspaper company in Paris—he was our employer for a time..." She faltered, closing her eyes for a second at the overwhelming tide of memories. *Monique. Harry. The beatings. The chilling screams.* She shivered delicately as they scrolled before her eyes and in her ears as if on a cinema screen. Her hands curled into fists as the familiar sense of helplessness knotted achingly in the hollow of her stomach.

"*Our*," Joe said. She blinked, unsure of what he was getting at. He elaborated, "You said '*our* employer'—did you work with Monique?"

"Not likely!" Louisa raised her eyebrows. "That spoiled madam never worked a day in her life!" She shook her head. "No, I worked with my...with

Harry." She swallowed the lump in her throat. "He died." Tugging a handkerchief from her pocket, she twisted it between her fingers.

Joe dropped his hands to his knees and leaned towards her, his expression sober. "You must miss him."

The compassion in his tone was almost her undoing. With an effort, she blinked away sudden tears. Hadn't she wept enough in the past five years?

"He was m…more than a colleague." She met his eyes. "You see, we…we were engaged to be married." Blowing her nose, she squared her shoulders and defiantly steeled her voice. "She sacrificed him to the Nazis and I'll *never* forgive her for that."

Joe looked stunned. "Engaged," he echoed, faintly.

"I have to find her, Joe. I've waited months for this." Louisa got to her feet. "And now it's come. The op is on hold; it's the chance I've been praying for."

"Whom do you have to find?" He scowled in sudden comprehension. "You don't mean that Monique woman?"

Louisa nodded. "She's the reason I'm here."

"But what do you plan to do with her?"

"I want to know why she did it." She stuffed her hanky back into her pocket. "Not knowing is tearing me apart."

Joe contemplated the floor. "So you want to interrogate her?" He flicked Louisa a critical glance. "That doesn't mean she'll give you any answers. And besides," he paused and his voice softened, "the truth can be hurtful. Are you prepared for that?"

Louisa swallowed and attempted a nonchalant shrug. Then, unable to ignore the challenge in his eyes, she huffed, "What makes you so darned sure that I won't like what I hear?"

"Experience has taught me—"

"In the school playground, was it?"

Joe pulled a face at her jibe. "You're not too old

for me to put you over my knee, young lady." Grinning wickedly, he began to rise.

She snorted. "Hah! I'd like to see you try." But she couldn't hide a giggle as he lunged for her. Laughingly fending him off, she cried out, "I'll behave, I'll behave!"

He settled back in his seat and began to roll himself another cigarette. "As it happens, it was a schoolmaster who impressed on me the painful truth." A shadow came into his eyes and Louisa felt a jolt of anxiety for him. Boys were caned for the slightest misdemeanors.

"What do you mean?"

He cleared his throat. "Dad was elected local district candidate to stand for parliament one year. Unfortunately for me, he was representing an earnest but unpopular party, which, as you can imagine, made me a target of every idiot bully around—and I don't just mean the other boys."

"The schoolmaster?"

Joe nodded. "Mr. Roberts was his name." He lit the cigarette. "One morning, at assembly, he made me defend my father's political opinions in front of the entire school. And then he announced that Dad was 'backing the wrong horse' and was a loser."

Louisa grimaced. "Cruel bastard!"

"Worst thing about it," Joe narrowed his eyes as he exhaled a thin plume of smoke, "was that he ended up being proved right. Truth is, Dad never did succeed in politics."

"I'd give your father credit for being willing to stand by his convictions and to give it a go."

Joe laughed grimly. "I did. But Dad was like a lamb to the slaughter! Never stood a cat in hell's—"

"I've made up my mind!" Louisa interrupted fiercely. "I don't need your approval. Maybe you think it's unwise," she tossed her head, "but you weren't there, you don't know how it feels to watch someone suffer as Harry did."

She pinched her lip to control her temper. The last thing she needed right now was for him to make her doubt herself, to scupper the plans she'd so carefully nurtured for years. She rose to leave the room.

"Lou...wait!" Joe leapt to his feet. "You can't handle this on your own, old girl." He rolled his eyes. "I know, call me old-fashioned..." His expression sobered. "But I'm coming with you."

She shook her head. "Thank you, but no, I'm perfectly capable of doing this alone. There's no point in you risking your neck for a cause that you don't believe in."

He fell silent for a second before briefly bending his knees to match her height. Holding her gaze, he murmured, "I believe in *you*."

Louisa's heart constricted. She hadn't expected this. She stared, tongue-tied as though all the words in her head had been suddenly blown away. No one, not even Harry, had ever said that they *believed* in her.

His gaze was sincere—her heart melted—so adorably sincere. As his thumbs began to feather-stroke the palms of her hands, her pulse raced and her toes curled in delicious expectation.

"Why?" She was curious to know more.

Teasingly, he invited, "Kiss me and I'll tell you."

His touch was hot. She gentled her mouth to his, skin upon skin, excited by the familiarity of his smoky scent. His tongue slipped to the edges of her lips, tempting her with waves of new, exquisite sensation, enticing her to open to him. A surge of liquid flame leapt between her legs.

His hand slipped from hers and moved to cup one breast, stroking, molding. As she inwardly squirmed with tortured passion, shafts of desire splintered through her and her legs trembled. As his kiss deepened, heat scorched her skin. Her heart thudded in her ears.

At the sound of car tires scrunching across the gravel, he broke the kiss with a reluctant groan. Wrapping his arms around her, he murmured in her ear, "I've never met another girl quite as unique as you."

"I did warn you." She chuckled.

"You did," he agreed. "You're exasperating, reckless—"

She interrupted with a gasp of outrage but he merely laughed and said, "But that bold spirit is why I believe in you." His gaze lingered. "Stay true to yourself, Lou, don't ever change."

She searched his face, her heart thumping fast at the realization that he, also, was very different. Most men's compliments were superficial—they told her what she could plainly see for herself by looking into a mirror. Joe saw her more deeply. He seemed to know what she needed to hear.

The honest respect in his eyes made her catch her breath. She knew, instinctively, that he'd be a faithful friend, just as he'd done his best to be a loyal son. His words weren't merely empty flattery designed to charm her into his bed.

She ached for him to kiss her again, but he took a step back, putting distance between them. His arms fell to his sides, but his gaze didn't waver. She forced herself to wait, struck by the powerful beauty of his manly face, unwilling to be the first to break the spell.

Finally, with a sigh of resignation, he said, "We may both be fighting for freedom, but you," he gathered one of her hands in his, "you, my pretty butterfly, even after this war is well over and done with, won't ever be free, will you, until you learn the truth?" He gave her a tender, pensive look. "So, all right, go alone, if you must. Go seek your peace. But," he released her hand and his tone hardened, "don't expect me to wait for you!"

Louisa's jaw dropped at this unexpected show of

defiance. But before she'd had a chance to reply, he'd stalked out of the room. She plucked at her bottom lip, unsettled by the fluttering panic in her chest. *Damn him.* He'd been so understanding, so darned *reasonable* about it but now that he was practically insisting that she be independent...a yawning chasm opened in her stomach. She'd planned everything in her head for months, always with the view of flying solo, never once had she factored in the possibility of anyone being willing to help...

Pressing her fingers to her temples, she realized that she couldn't recall another time when she'd been thrown into such a flurry of indecision. Maybe she'd been too hasty. She had no idea how long she would be away, but it was more than likely he'd not be here when she returned.

If she returned.

She gulped in a breath. Anything could happen to either of them. But... it was too late to change her mind. If she backed down now, he would never take her seriously again.

A rap on the door interrupted her muse. Ace called out his password and she ran to let him in. He took off his cap with one hand and ran a finger around the back of his collar. Shaking out a red handkerchief to wipe his brow, he complained, "It's getting mighty warm out there." He studied Louisa from under his auburn tipped eyebrows. "Any news of Claude?" She shook her head in reply and Ace said, "I've a message from Dickie—he wants ya to meet him in the village."

Louisa sighed with relief at the confirmation that Dickie was alive and well. Claude had tried to trick her but she'd also feared that Dickie had gotten into difficulties after Joe had seen him with Monique.

"What time?"

"Just as soon as I can get ya there."

Heart skipping a beat, Louisa seized the

opportunity to keep her pride intact and shouted, "Joe! Did you hear that? Dickie wants to see us."

Ace put a restraining hand on her arm. "No, ma'am. Only you."

"He's my responsibility, you said." Ignoring Ace's gesture, she gathered up her coat and bags. "I'm not leaving him here alone."

Ace bent toward her as though he was about to argue, but said nothing as Joe, shooting Louisa a bemused glance, entered the room.

The rain had completely cleared and the sun was pushing the remaining clouds aside. As they motored towards the village centre, it glinted brightly off muddy puddles in the road.

Ace dropped them at the corner, pointing out the café.

"I know the place," said Louisa, recognizing it from the night before. It was where she'd seen Claude meet with Alain. As she and Joe approached, it suddenly struck her as peculiar that Claude had so desperately wanted that money. Surely he was making plenty from his business deals. It was common knowledge that people were prepared to pay outrageous amounts for illegal black market goods.

She shrugged off her concerns. He was probably living beyond his means and was in debt. She grimaced, remembering the hotel. Prostitutes were expensive, no doubt.

Louisa pushed open the café's heavy wooden door. The place was humming with lunchtime patrons. Cigarette smoke curled thickly above their heads. Hesitating long enough to allow her eyes to adjust to the gloom, she went in, Joe following close behind. Dickie, pipe wedged between his teeth, was sitting at a table in the far corner. He waved them over and greeted them in French.

Louisa was prepared to explain Joe's presence, but Dickie didn't ask. Ace must have briefed him on Joe's change of plan. He seemed preoccupied, moodily staring into space. When the waiter brought over three coffees, she realized that Dickie had even pre-ordered.

She took a sip from the cup in front of her and pulled a face. It tasted foul.

"Au lait?" suggested Dickie, cradling his pipe in one hand and pushing the jug of milk towards her with the other. "You'll find that it makes the stuff somewhat more palatable." He signaled the waiter. "Another coffee, s'il vous plait?"

"No need," Louisa protested. "I'll try it your way."

Dickie shook his head. "I wasn't expecting..." he indicated Joe, "You see..." He glanced towards the door and smiled. "Ah! Here she is."

He'd set up a rendezvous with someone? Louisa cursed under her breath. Now she'd not be able to have the private conversation she'd been hoping for. Forcing a polite smile, she looked in the direction in which Dickie had turned.

"Bonjour!" A familiar, high-pitched voice.

The smile froze on her lips. *Mon Dieu!* What the hell was Monique doing here?

"Lulu! When I heard you were back I simply *had* to come from Paris to make sure wiz my very own eyes."

Stunned into silence, Louisa heard the air kissed somewhere near her cheek. She breathed in a familiar perfume and cringed inwardly as she watched a dazzling smile being unleashed in Joe's direction. *Butter wouldn't melt...* She glared at Dickie. *How could you?*

Dickie avoided making eye contact. Twiddling one end of his moustache, he introduced Monique to Joe.

"Enchanté," she purred, smiling flirtatiously. She sat and unbuttoned her black fur coat to expose a cream silk blouse. She fingered the string of pearls around her neck and adjusted one of the matching earrings.

Louisa sent Joe a warning glance, worried that his accent would give him away. But he merely smiled politely and said nothing. Louisa, quickly scanning the other tables, was relieved to note that all the other patrons seemed to be minding their own business.

She narrowed her eyes. Of even greater threat was the woman now sitting opposite Joe. Meeting her in this way was unexpected. She'd not had time to prepare.

Trepidation shivered through her but she reminded herself she'd learned from the past. If Monique expected Louisa to have forgiven and forgotten, then more fool her.

As another coffee arrived, Dickie began some small talk. Though Monique appeared to be listening, Louisa watched her hazel eyes sending flirty looks across the table. *A leopard never changes its spots.*

"I heard what happened last night." Dickie turned his attention to Louisa. "It got a little dirty?" He gestured with his pipe to the bruise on her face.

She shrugged, but said nothing.

"I've seen worse." Monique flicked them a look that Louisa couldn't quite decipher.

"Coffee is on ze 'ouse." Alain approached the table and smiled a welcome.

"Non, non!" protested Dickie politely—but Alain insisted.

Monique excused herself to go to the powder room. As soon as she was out of earshot, Louisa turned crossly to Dickie and said in French, "Why didn't you warn me?"

Dickie clenched his pipe between his teeth. "But darling, didn't Ace mention she'd be here?"

"No, he damned well didn't!" Louisa crossed her arms over her chest. "But now that she is, I want a private meeting with her."

Dickie removed his pipe and frowned with suspicion. "No. I absolutely forbid it."

Joe asked her what he'd said. Louisa could have hugged him when, turning to Dickie, he insisted in a low, firm voice, "She knows what she's doing."

When Monique returned, Louisa inquired mildly, "Are you visiting for the day or will you be staying longer?"

"I'll be back on ze train just as soon as I've sorted out some business." Monique, avoiding Louisa's scrutiny, picked up her starched napkin and dabbed at the sides of her mouth.

Louisa glanced at Dickie. All the color had drained from his face. What exactly was Monique's business? Suddenly she realized that the whole café had gone quiet. Everyone seemed to be frozen into silence, like children playing a game of Statues.

Behind her, the café door closed with a resounding click and there was a scuffle of boots against the wooden floor. Alain scurried over to greet his customer. Louisa glanced over her shoulder. Her stomach clenched painfully—it was the ugly gendarme she'd encountered the previous night.

Louisa caught Dickie's eye. Indicating her bruise, she hissed, "*Merde!* It's him!"

Chapter Nine

Dickie took charge. Briskly assisting an astonished Monique to her feet, he announced loudly, "Come, *chérie*. You are very ill. We must find a doctor. You might be contagious…" Ignoring her strident protests, he scooped her into his arms and strode towards the back entrance.

The effect of his words was like a match to dry grass. The café sprang into life as a ripple of speculative chatter erupted throughout the room. The mention of illness caused instant panic. The gendarme immediately found his progress blocked as people tried to leave en masse.

"Might be polio!"

"Could be tuberculosis…"

"My neighbor lost her son to influenza…"

The gendarme shouted out orders for calm but his words fell on deaf ears. Jostling and elbowing, everyone tried to exit at once.

Louisa grabbed Joe and made for the kitchen. Dodging the agitated chef and his assistant, she opened the door into the alley and motioned to Joe to follow her to the street. They merged with the customers at the front exit and crossed to the other side.

Too late, Louisa noticed the gendarme approaching but, fortunately, his attention remained focused on the group behind them. She caught Joe's sleeve. "Kiss me. *Now!*"

In less urgent circumstances, Joe's astonished expression would've caused her to laugh, but he did as she wished.

To her huge relief, the gendarme hurried by

without even a glance. *Just an anonymous pair of young lovers.*

"I think you're learning the ways of a Frenchman," she whispered, reluctantly unsealing their lips.

"I need more practice," he murmured, his arms tightening around her.

With a chuckle, she lightly pushed him away and quickly scanned the area for a glimpse of Dickie. It was fruitless. The streets had emptied.

She tucked her hand under Joe's arm and together they strode quickly up to a small boutique. Under the faded green and white striped window awning stood a bench seat.

"Wait here and watch for Dickie," instructed Louisa. "I'll be right back."

She ducked inside. Shopping would be a legitimate way to keep out of sight. She greeted the shop assistant and, her mind racing, pretended to browse through the clothing racks.

She longed to find out what Monique was up to. She was here for a reason and Louisa was prepared to bet that it was not an innocent one. Dickie had appeared as shocked as she at Monique's reference to "taking care of business." Louisa felt convinced that the Frenchwoman's visit was much more than a social catch-up.

****

Joe sat on the warm wooden slats and rolled himself a cigarette. The afternoon sun dazzled low under the awning. To shade his eyes, he tweaked the peak of his cap down almost to the tip of his nose. His heartbeat was still going nineteen-to-the-dozen. He wasn't sure what had happened back in the café, but it was obvious it had something to do with that policeman and something else to do with that woman, Monique.

He looked both ways down the street. A bare-footed young boy squeaked by, laboriously peddling an ancient, rusted bicycle.

The heat made Joe sleepy. Yawning, he threw his cigarette butt onto the cobbles and stubbed it out with his foot. He glanced at his watch and shifted his position on the seat. He crossed and uncrossed his legs. Why was Louisa taking so long?

Swiveling round to the window behind him, Joe pressed his face close to the glass, using one hand to shield the glare. He could see her at the back of the narrow shop, engaged in conversation with someone. He glanced over the few racks of clothes. It was a strange assortment—more like costume or fancy dress than high fashion.

He didn't hear the soft steps beside him. He did not see the shadow which formed across his back. But at the light touch on his shoulder, he swung around, heart in his mouth. He should have been watching...

"M'sieur?"

Joe squinted at the shoeless figure and let out a sigh of relief. It was the lad he had just seen cycling past.

"M'sieur." He beckoned Joe to follow him.

Joe hesitated.

"The mademoiselle...!" The lad's voice rose in agitation as he pointed towards the shop.

Something was wrong? Joe hurried to follow the boy up the street and around the corner.

His pace slowed as he spied Louisa at the end of a narrow service entrance. As he drew closer, she began to strap a covered wicker basket onto the front of a ladies' bicycle. Intrigued, Joe raised an eyebrow. What had she purchased?

"Can you ride a bike?" she asked. The lad's bicycle was propped against the wall.

"Not that old thing?" He pulled a face.

She grinned. "It'll save time. We have to go to the station."

"Why?"

"Call it a hunch."

Joe, fearing it would be a miracle if the bike made it there in one piece, gingerly saddled the seat. It tipped alarmingly as he lowered his full weight onto it but after an initial wobble or two and more than a few disturbing squeaks, he managed to follow in Louisa's wake.

****

Louisa peddled vigorously across the worn cobbles and felt every single bump. The contents of the basket may have jiggled right out of the top if not held down by the cover. She could hear Joe's cycle, the noise getting louder and faster as he drew parallel with her. She glanced at him. He was grimacing with the effort or maybe because of the excruciating noise. He certainly didn't look comfortable.

Catching his eye, she pointed ahead to the turn-off. Coasting together down the gentle slope, they skidded to a halt beside the rail terminal. Louisa leaned her bike against the wall and retrieved her package from the basket as Joe propped his bike against hers. They stepped onto the platform. The train was idling a few yards away.

"Do you still have your ticket?"

"Yes." Joe checked his pocket.

"Keep your eyes peeled for Monique."

Louisa purchased a ticket from the small office and strode quickly beside the carriages, glancing into each one. She halted suddenly. Her instinct had been correct. "There she is on the far side." She looked around. "I wonder if Dickie is here somewhere."

Joe made to put a foot on the first step.

"Wait a minute." Louisa had sighted Dickie up ahead just as the station guard was making his way down the length of the train.

Dickie quickened his stride, waving a rolled-up newspaper to catch their attention.

The train whistle blew loud in their ears.

"Hurry, Lou," urged Joe. "We can't wait for him."

Leaping on a second before the carriage doors closed, Louisa turned to see Dickie's face at the window. He was trying to say something. Louisa shook her head in dismay.

The train lurched forward. Dickie ran along beside, pointing into the carriage while mouthing words through the glass. Louisa threw her hands up in silent frustration and Dickie clutched the top of his head with both hands in a gesture of despair.

She realized that he was trying to tell them something important, but it was impossible to make out. With a huff of resignation, she took off her kitbag and placed it—and the package—under her feet.

Joe eyed the brown paper with its binding of string. "What's in there?"

With a grin, she said, "Something for you."

He raised an eyebrow. "Am I going to like it?"

She merely laughed at his wary tone and turned her attention to their fellow passengers. This end of the carriage was virtually empty. Monique was sitting up front, along with the bulk of the other travelers.

Louisa glanced back at Joe. He was gazing out the window, seemingly engrossed in the rows of apple trees parading along the passing green landscape.

"Joe?" She snuggled her head against his shoulder and yawned. She remembered that she hadn't had much rest the night before. The rocking of the train soothed her.

As he turned his head, she glanced up at him to touch his cheek with her fingers.

He clasped her hand and brought it to his lips. His kiss warmed her palm. "Hmm?" he prompted.

"Keep an eye on Monique, will you?"

He searched her face. "Does this mean...?"

"Oui," she murmured sleepily. "I can't do this alone." Her head lolled forward onto his chest and she mumbled, "Don't let her out of your sight."

****

She needed him. She'd actually admitted it. Joe smiled as he placed Louisa's hand gently back on her lap. Shifting himself into a more comfortable position, he placed an arm around her shoulders and drew her closer. She was obviously exhausted, poor old girl. Stretching his legs a little, he tried to ease the tension from his body.

A man sitting on the other side of the carriage caught his eye. His leathery face was crinkled with age. He spoke in rapid French to Joe and winked.

Joe smiled politely. He could only guess at what the old devil was saying. To forestall the possibility of him expecting a reply, Joe pointed at the sleeping Louisa and put a finger to his lips.

The elderly bloke's wide smile revealed gap-toothed gums. He adjusted his motley beret, shrugged bony shoulders and, to Joe's relief, turned away.

Joe knew he must stay alert. To divert his thoughts from the distraction of Louisa, so warm and inviting in his arms, he focused on the back of Monique's blonde head. Her black fur hat was perfectly poised on top of her neatly coiled hair. Although he couldn't tell from where he was sitting, he felt sure that not a wisp of hair was out of place. With her elegant neck the color of porcelain, she was like a doll that had never been taken out of its box.

He glanced down at Louisa's tousled curls. His gaze skimmed over her smudged coat, scuffed shoes and battle-scarred bag. The phrase 'dragged through a hedge backwards' came into his mind, and his lips twitched in silent amusement. She couldn't be more different from Monique if she tried.

His gaze flicked back to the woman. He wondered if she had seen them enter the carriage, but the dozen or so people sitting in-between them had probably blocked her view. She had certainly not given any indication that she was aware of their presence.

Louisa's head pressed into his chest. He realized that he had no idea how long the journey would be. The setting sun colored the sky with tangerine and pink before the features of the countryside blurred into a cobalt blue dusk. He rubbed his eyes with his free hand, closing them for just an instant.

He woke, startled, to see that Monique had stood up to lift something down from the overhead luggage rack. The train was slowing down. Had they reached Paris? He ducked his head as she turned in their direction. Had she seen him?

****

Louisa's arm quivered. A groan escaped her lips as she tried to bury herself back into sleep. The pressure on her arm tightened, like the clamp of a steel band. A demanding voice growled in her ear, "Wake up, Lou."

She opened her eyes. For a minute she was confused, disorientated. She blinked. But as the train's squealing brakes loudly assaulted her ears, she hastily hauled herself upright.

Joe heaved the parcel into her lap, picked up her kitbag and got to his feet, bracing himself against the movement of the slowing train.

"We can't be in Paris yet," she protested. Joe stared past her. His guilty expression surely meant only one thing—he had lost Monique. *Merde!*

Chapter Ten

"Ve meet again, Fraulein."

The clipped accent sent off warning bells in Louisa's head. Tightening her hold on the parcel, she rose to her feet. Turning to face the speaker, prickles raced along her spine as she recognized the German officer who'd led the raid on the cottage. She gripped the back of the seat.

"I see that your foot is healed now," he said.

"Oui. Merci." She gave him a fake smile.

"Are you alighting here?"

She glanced ahead to where she had last seen Monique. To her relief, she spotted her making her way towards the forward exit. She turned back to the German officer and nodded curtly. "Oui." She took a step towards him. "Excusez moi, s'il vous plait."

"One moment." He raised a hand in a gesture of stopping her progress.

Louisa's heart thumped. *Get out of our way.* It was imperative she not lose Monique. Every second was a delay she couldn't afford.

His eyes assessed her before his gaze flicked to Joe, standing stiffly behind her. For one heart-stopping second she thought the officer was going to speak to him. If Joe attempted a reply, his stumbling French would be a dead giveaway.

Quickly, she asked, "Did you find the missing airman?" She flashed the officer another pert smile.

He puffed out his chest and replied smugly, "Ja." *Yes.* "Ve have captured many airmen."

The old man was trying to squeeze past. He coughed croakily, as if full of phlegm. The officer pulled a face of disgust, saluted "Heil Hitler!" and hurriedly stood aside.

Louisa caught Joe's eye as they stumbled onto the platform. He was looking as relieved as she felt. Dressed in French clothing, his disguise had failed to arouse suspicion.

"Where are we?" he asked. "This doesn't look like the city."

"I don't know." As the train chugged away, she glanced about. There was no signboard. "But," she agreed, "it certainly isn't Paris."

As Monique strode toward the end of the station, Louisa began to follow but abruptly stopped as she saw her pause and bend forward. Quickly, she pulled Joe into the shadows of the overhead shelter.

As a wisp of cigarette smoke curled above her head, Monique straightened up and continued walking.

Maintaining a discreet distance, Louisa and Joe followed her out into the empty countryside. Blackness soon enfolded them and they could only be guided by the sound of Monique's shoes crunching on the gravel road.

Louisa swapped the parcel to her other arm. She looked into the sky. It was a clear, star-twinkling night. With eyes now adjusting to the dark, she used the moon's glow to pinpoint Monique more firmly in her sights.

"Ssshh." Joe came to a standstill.

Louisa's fingers tightened on Joe's arm. She couldn't make out the expression on his face but the tension in his arm muscles signaled a warning. She looked ahead but could only see Monique walking along as before.

"What is it?"

"Ssshh," he repeated, more loudly this time.

"I'm not deaf."

"You must be. Listen!"

She lifted her chin, her eyes widening at the

glow of light swaying ahead of Monique. At the same moment, she heard a distant, rhythmic squeaking.

"Someone's coming. Get down!"

From her crouched position, she heard the muffled rumble of a man's voice. She watched as the lantern rose above Monique's head.

Hardly daring to breathe, Louisa strained to hear what was being said, but the voices were too low. The squeaking of the swinging handle grew louder.

"Quick. Through here!" Joe crawled through a gap in the hedge and held back his hand to help her. Louisa followed.

The lantern cast a glow over where they had just been, hesitated, and then continued on and away in the direction of the station.

Louisa let out a long, slow breath of relief and crept back onto the road. Monique had advanced well ahead, but there was just enough moon to spotlight her honey-colored hair, so that it shone like a beacon. As Monique turned into a driveway lined with trees, Louisa stifled a gasp of recognition. Why hadn't she realized before?

Turning to Joe, she whispered, "I know where we are. See that?" She pointed to the large building in the distance. "That's a beautiful chateau where I spent some happy times before the war. Monique's parents own it."

Louisa turned into the drive. The towering trees obliterated the moonlight so that it was suddenly opaquely black. She hesitated. She could hear Joe's footsteps then felt him bump into her. She heard his soft apology. Up ahead, Monique had disappeared.

She fought down a rising panic as something fluttered in the trees above. "Joe?" She took a step backwards.

Joe steadied her against him. "It's just a bat."

She edged a foot forward as the blackness enfolded her like a smothering blanket. She sucked in a deep breath and then another, fighting the urge to halt—she knew the way to the chateau and could rely on her memory to guide them.

"Hold on a minute," Joe said softly. He struck a match. The sizzle of light briefly illuminated the path ahead before plunging them back into darkness.

Louisa blinked. Now everything seemed even blacker than before.

The rumbling of a motorcar startled her. Confused, she tried to pinpoint the direction of the sound. She stifled a gasp as an arm encircled her waist and wrenched her under the trees.

She listened as the car's engine got louder. Joe had pulled her out of the way in the nick of time. From their hiding place she watched it purr slowly on past, its dimmed headlights weak. But there was enough illumination for Louisa to see a flag bearing a swastika on the bonnet and that the three occupants wore German officers' caps. *Mon Dieu! Why were they going to the chateau?*

Distracted by this new information, she didn't pay any attention to the whooshing sound above her. Just another bat. Her arm reached out for Joe, waving blindly in the dark.

"Joe?" Her arm fell into empty space. "Where...?" The words died on her lips as a hand clamped firmly across her mouth. The last thing she heard was the dull thump of something solid connecting with the back of her head.

****

A high-pitched moaning echoed in her ears. It seemed to be coming from far away. Louisa struggled to open her eyes a crack. Where was she? She flinched at the strong light as her tongue flicked across dry lips. The moaning came closer, increasing in volume. She tried to raise her head but it was too heavy. Then she realized the sound came from her own mouth.

"Lou?"

"Joe?" Her voice croaked. She shielded her eyes against the glare with one hand. "What happened?"

"I think someone clobbered us. We're somewhere inside the chateau." He wriggled a little closer to where she lay on the floor. "I guess your head is as sore as mine."

She tried to sit up but the effort made her head swim with dizziness. She put out a hand to touch him. "Are you all in one piece?"

"Think so."

From her prone position, she could see they were in a round room completely bare of furniture. The light source was a small, oblong, leadlight window. It was sunlight. She must have been unconscious for hours.

She glimpsed a patch of blue sky, but no trees. That could mean they were on one of the upper floors. Louisa knew there were many rooms in the chateau but with the sun in the position that it was she surmised they were somewhere in the east wing. She shifted uncomfortably on the hard wooden floor and turned her head to look for her kitbag. It, along with the parcel, was lying on the other side of Joe.

Louisa eased a hand into the pocket of her coat. The revolver was gone. A wave of nausea overwhelmed her and she heaved herself away from Joe, rolling onto her side and retching over the dusty floorboards.

She lay back, exhausted, craving a drink of water. She moaned again and felt his hand catch hers.

"How long...have we been here?"

Joe gently squeezed. "Most of the night. I only awoke just before you did." He glanced at his watch. "It's just after nine."

"Have you checked the door?"

Joe eased himself into a sitting position. He gingerly probed the tender spot on the back of his head and then stood up. Swaying slightly, he put his hand out to steady himself before making his way to the door. He tried the handle. It was locked.

Louisa sat up as Joe plopped back down beside her.

"Monique must have seen us last night." Joe drew his knees up, placed his elbows on them and cupped his head in his hands.

"Even if she did, she couldn't have knocked us out and dragged us up here on her own. She must have had help."

"Maybe the lantern-bearer?"

"Or whoever she was planning on meeting here."

"Those officers?" Joe turned to look at her, his eyebrows raised.

At that moment, there was a scuffling sound outside the door. The key turned in the lock and the door swung open.

"I trust you slept well." Monique, panting slightly, strode in and shut the door behind her. She appraised them equally, smiling as if greeting long-awaited guests.

Louisa shot her what she hoped was a withering look. "What do you want with us?"

Monique arched one elegant eyebrow. "What do *I* want? It's not as simple as zat."

Louisa choked back another surge of nausea. Did Monique know what she and Dickie were involved in? If so, how? Dickie would never have breached their security. But there must be some reason for treating them like this—did it have to do with those officers or had they somehow been set up for more personal reasons? Had they unwittingly walked into some kind of trap?

"I'll have some food brought up to you. After zat, we'll talk!" Monique left the room, locking the door behind her once more.

Joe half-filled a bowl with water from a large jug standing near the window. He splashed some across his face. There was no towel, so he dried himself with a corner of his shirt. Picking up an old chipped mug, he filled it with water and drank thirstily. He rinsed it and refilled it to take to Louisa. As he passed the window, he glanced down but immediately pulled back with a sharp intake of breath.

"What is it?" Louisa asked, alarmed.

"It's a hell of a long way down." He shuddered.

Louisa wondered if he was unwell but all she said was, "Yes, judging by the shape of the room, I think we must be in one of the towers."

He passed a hand across his forehead as if trying to ease an ache. "Do you have any *Aspro*?"

Louisa pulled a small bottle out of her bag. She handed the bottle to him with one hand while rubbing the back of her neck with the other. If only she'd had her wee pillow to soften the effect of the hard floor, not to mention the effect of that thump, she thought.

Joe downed a couple of the small white pills, swilling them down with more water. He offered them to Louisa but she shook her head as she tucked the bottle back into her bag. To her surprise, he knelt behind her and began to knead the back of her neck with his fingers.

His hands slipped down under her coat to her shoulders. "That any better?" He pressed the ball of his thumbs along her shoulder blades in a soothing, rhythmic motion.

She let out a contented sigh and relaxed against the steadying push of his hands. As his fingers probed more deeply, the pain slowly ebbed away, allowing her to concentrate on thinking up an escape plan. Monique had said that food would be coming, so they could possibly use that opportunity to slip through the door. Then it would be a simple matter of negotiating several flights of stairs to the ground floor.

She closed her eyes and tried to visualize the plan of the building as she remembered it. She frowned slightly as she realized that she'd never actually ventured any further up than the second floor before. The towers were rarely used as far as she knew. In the days when she had stayed as the weekend guest of Monique's parents, she'd never even given the towers a second thought—they were simply decorative.

Her frown deepened. Joe was right—they were also a very, very long way up. Why had she and Joe been hauled way up here when there were plenty of other rooms they could have been held in, most of which were hardly ever occupied?

Joe had released the pressure and was trying to push her coat off. "Oh, please don't stop," she pleaded.

"My fingers are going numb," he explained. "It'll be easier without it."

She shrugged out of her coat and undid the top buttons of her next layer. His fingers brushed against her neck.

"Good, eh?" He kneaded his hands down over the skin of her shoulders until she was almost purring with contentment.

Louisa's eyes glazed in a daydream of reminiscence. She was singing and laughing at the pre-war winter parties, warmed by the chunky logs blazing and crackling in the huge fireplace on the chateau's ground floor.

"I had my first dance with Harry here," she murmured. "He was quite a catch. All the girls longed to be his beau." She gave him a wry smile. "Monique was horribly envious."

"He was after both of you, eh? I've heard of the French males' reputation," Joe muttered.

"Oh, but he wasn't French." Louisa twisted around to face him. "He was a New Zealander." She added unnecessarily, "Like you."

Joe blinked, then understanding lit his eyes. "I had wondered how you'd recognized my accent."

Rattle, clunk. The door opened and food on a tray was pushed into the room. Louisa scrambled to her feet and lunged at the door. Too late, the door clicked shut.

"Let us out!" Her fists hammered at the heavy wood. She twisted the handle but it wouldn't budge. She crouched to peer through the keyhole. "*Merde!*"

"I suggest you eat some of this." Joe picked up the tray. "We'll need to build up our strength if we're to have a chance of getting out of this place."

She glanced at him with a twinge of regret. She should never have involved him. "Joe?" She caught his gaze and drew in a breath. "If anything should happen to me, if we're separated, I want you to promise that you'll put yourself first."

A muscle in his cheek twitched. "But we're a team, aren't we?"

Her heart flipped. She couldn't bear to think of anything happening to him.

"Please..."

He shrugged. "Stop worrying. It won't come to that." He set the tray firmly in front of her and sat down.

She eyed him doubtfully but decided not to push it. They shared the bread and sliced meat between them and washed it down with more water. Then Louisa walked over to the window, rolling her head from side to side and scrunching up her shoulders as she went. "I feel much better." She flashed Joe a grateful smile. "Thanks."

She glanced out the window for a long moment before wriggling the metal latch. To her surprise it swung open, leaving a gap she estimated would be just big enough to squeeze through, if they had to. She leaned over the sill to assess the balcony below. It was a long way down—far too risky to jump. She closed the window again. There had to be another way.

Joe paced the room like a caged lion. He was obviously feeling better and ready for action.

"Any suggestions?" he asked.

"We've got to get out before we are questioned."

He shot her a wry smile. "You have a plan?"

"Monique indicated that there are others interested in us—presumably the officers that we saw last night. However, I've just seen them driving away—must have been called to something more important." She fell into step beside him. "Chances are she's here on her own, so with a bit of luck, we could turn this to our advantage." She moved to her kitbag and took out a penknife. Then she knelt by the door and began to pick the lock.

Joe raised an eyebrow. "Where did you learn that trick, or shouldn't I ask?"

"Definitely hush-hush," Louisa agreed with a quick grin.

She surveyed the hallway. At least there was no guard. She stopped to listen for footsteps.

She turned to Joe who had gathered up the parcel and bags. Shouldering her kitbag on one arm, she said, "This way." They turned left down the small hallway and began to descend the steep spiral staircase.

Their footsteps echoed eerily against the cold stone walls. The only light came from regularly placed narrow slits, through which cold draughts of air fanned them as they passed. Louisa put her hands out to the sides to steady herself as she placed each foot carefully on the narrow treads. Peering ahead into the gloom, she could just make out a dark wooden door. It had a high, narrow window with black bars across it.

A shiver ran down her spine as she negotiated the final step at the bottom of the tower but whether it was from fear, or from the cold chill in the air, she couldn't tell. Joe squeezed into the narrow space beside her, his warm bulk pressing against her hip. Pausing briefly to listen, she turned the heavy iron handle, pulling the door open towards them. She edged around it, with Joe following closely and blinked her eyes at the sudden dazzle of bright light streaming in through the large, magnificent leadlight windows on either side of the wide corridor. With a sense of relief, Louisa closed the heavy door against the gloom behind them. They had made it to the second floor.

"So far, so good." Joe's voice was in her ear.

She moved swiftly towards the wide staircase, feeling thankful that she'd remembered the layout of this part of the building.

If they could just sneak downstairs without being seen, then they'd reach plenty of places to hide. Joe adjusted the parcel he'd tucked under one arm.

They had just about reached the bottom when Monique stepped forward from the side where she'd been hidden from their view.

"Leaving us already?" She held Louisa's gun at arm's length in front of her. "Zat is hardly polite." A sarcastic smirk sidled across her mouth. "Did you not appreciate ze hospitality?"

Chapter Eleven

Louisa, heart pounding, clutched the banister. "What do you want with us?"

Monique kept the gun trained in their direction. "Sit down, on your hands!" She waited as Louisa and Joe obeyed, then lowered the gun and said, "I'll ask the questions, s'il vous plait." Her voice hardened. "Why did you follow me here?"

Louisa's eyes narrowed. "You surely know that we have unfinished business."

"I can hardly zink what!"

But Louisa saw a flicker of fear in her eyes. Chancing a brief surveillance of the elegant reception room, she was immediately drawn to the evidence of the new occupants—a large, framed photograph of Hitler above the mantel.

She glanced back at Monique. "How are your parents, by the way?"

"Zey understand zat it is better to co-operate zan to lose everyzing."

"I can't believe that your father would collaborate. Surely, keeping his reputation—"

"My family has done what zey have had to do!" She took a step towards Louisa, her eyes bulging in anger. "Have you come to make trouble?"

"Ha!" Louisa curled her lip. "Why didn't you get help for Harry? How could you leave him to those Nazi brutes?" Her breath came out in short gasps. She rose to her feet. "You traitor!"

Monique glared as though she was about to burst a blood vessel with fury. She advanced, gun aimed, her finger tightening on the trigger. But the sudden sound of approaching footsteps alerted them all to the fact that their raised voices had attracted interest.

A giant of a man came into view. His neck was as thick as a tree trunk and his broad chest strained against the metal buttons of his uniform jacket.

"Take zem back to the tower!" Monique screeched.

Joe leapt up, distracting Monique. Louisa kicked the gun out of her hands. As it spun away, Louisa dived for it. Twisting her body in a half-turn, she aimed it at the giant's head just as he was about to clamp his meaty hands around Joe's ears.

She fired. The large man fell, missing Joe by only a hair's breadth. Monique started to back away but Joe grabbed her.

Louisa glared as Monique squirmed against Joe's grip. Addressing her in English so that Joe could understand, Louisa spat, "You don't deserve to live."

The panic in the woman's eyes fueled Louisa's rage, even as her conscience was horrified by it. But her anger had been contained for so long, so very long. Somehow she had to find the courage to do this for Harry—it was the only chance to make it up to him, to fulfil the promise she'd made to herself. If she blew this opportunity, how could she ever forgive herself for her weakness?

At this sobering thought, her heart hardened into ice. She gave full vent to her bitterness. "You should die in agony—to suffer as much as Harry did!"

Louisa could sense Joe's shock at her words, but she had no regrets. She meant every single one.

Monique tried to buck herself out of Joe's arms, but Joe tightened his grip. Placing the gun on the floor, Louisa stooped and stripped the dead man of his trouser belt before indicating to Joe to spin Monique around so she could tie her hands.

"Let me go!" Monique turned her pleading gaze

toward Joe. "Zis wing of ze chateau has been commandeered by ze Boche. Get out now—while you can."

"Bitch!" Louisa yanked the belt tight.

Monique yelped in pain.

Louisa retrieved the gun and pulled Monique back around to face her. "Collaborating with the enemy justifies your death."

"No!" Monique cried. "My parents rely on me. Papa was forced to hand over zis part of ze chateau."

"And what about Harry? Were you forced to hand him over?" Louisa jammed the gun hard against Monique's head. Her hand shook, though she tried to steady herself.

As Monique flinched in Joe's arms, he called out, "Louisa! Show some mercy."

Her scrutiny never wavered. "Did she show mercy when Harry was being attacked? When he was beaten so badly that the flesh was almost hanging off his bones?"

Monique glanced away.

"Look at me!" Louisa lifted a hand and slapped Monique, once, twice, across the face.

"I—I didn't know zat zey would k...kill him!" Monique's eyes moistened. She glanced at the lifeless body at her feet and sniffed. "I thought they'd only f...frighten him...into leaving P...Paris." She shuddered. "Don't hurt me!"

"For God's sake, Louisa," implored Joe. "Think what you're doing...this is murder!"

"Why should I?" Louisa's lips twisted disdainfully at Monique's blatant self-pity. "Harry was innocent. He didn't deserve what happened to him."

"What good will it do to harm her? Two wrongs don't make a right."

She snorted with derision at the cliché. Monique was a vain, selfish, spiteful woman, used to getting her own way. Louisa flashed Joe an irritable glance and caught the discomfort in his eyes.

She hesitated. *Darn him!* Maybe he was right. Perhaps that's what divided them from the monsters in this war. To show mercy would be more than *they* would do.

Tension stretched between them like a taut rubber band. Monique's face paled chalky white, her pupils dilated with horror.

Louisa glanced quickly towards the doors, aware that they could be disturbed at any moment. There was no more time to pursue further answers. She narrowed her eyes. Possibly Monique had been punished enough. After a second, Louisa defied her better judgement and reluctantly lowered the gun.

As Monique sagged with relief, she warned, "One chance only. And it's far more than you deserve." She indicated the dead man. "Where can we hide...?"

"Under ze stairs!"

Louisa said briskly, "Untie her, Joe. It'll take all three of us to shift the body."

They heaved and grunted with the effort of moving the heavy man. Louisa opened the stair cupboard door, then darted back to quickly roll up the bloodstained rug. They shoved both into the dark cubby hole. Just as Louisa was about to shut the door, a stored box of ammunition caught her eye.

The sudden sound of car tires crunching on the gravel outside had them all glancing towards the main entrance.

"*Merde!* Where can we hide?" Louisa slammed the cupboard door and looked around. She knew that one of the doors led to the kitchens and another to the dining room.

"Not here," Monique hissed. "Ze tower is ze only safe place. No one goes up zere."

"Come on!" Louisa turned and led the way. Joe scooped up the parcel he'd dropped and grabbed Monique firmly by the elbow. They ran up the stairs, disappearing around the corner of the landing just as they heard the sound of boots and men's voices approaching on the lower floor. Then they fled back up the narrow, twisting stairway.

****

Now what? Joe thought, as he dropped the parcel and leaned, chest heaving, against the doorframe. He checked his watch. The whole day was still ahead of them. He hoped they wouldn't have to spend it shut up in this small room. He glanced at Louisa but she was keeping a wary eye on Monique.

He stretched out a leg and poked the parcel with his foot. He'd been carrying the darn thing around all this time without any idea of what was in it. It had felt soft and quite heavy in his arms.

Curious, he leaned forward to untie the string but was prevented by Louisa's foot clamping down on it. He looked up in surprise. She shook her head. "Not yet."

He gazed back at her shoe and admired the slender shapeliness of her ankle. If he reached out, he could stroke her leg right up under her skirt and touch the delicate soft skin hidden there. Memories of her sweet kisses were still fresh. With an inward sigh, he dug a hand in his pocket and pulled out his tobacco pouch.

"When the time's right..." Louisa glanced at him with a look of amusement.

He stared at her. Had she known what he was thinking about? Then he realized that she was referring to the parcel. Feeling a little foolish, he bent to hide his grin and began to roll a cigarette.

****

Louisa addressed Monique, "How can we get out of here?"

"At twelve o'clock zey will all be at luncheon in ze dining hall," she replied, her tone sullen.

Louisa checked her watch. "That's ten minutes

away."

Monique eyed Louisa. "Zey will be expecting me—"

"A business lunch, I suppose?"

Monique, defying Louisa's sarcasm, lifted her chin proudly. "France needs Germany to win zis war. It will be our way to a better future."

"You little fool!" Louisa spat out the words. "The Nazis have murdered thousands. You think they have France's interests at heart? They will make slaves of us all. Only the Fatherland matters to them. How could you want that?"

"Zat's not what zey have promised. Papa will be able to expand ze printing business."

"If there's anyone qualified left to work for him." Louisa's voice was heavy with cynicism. "Look what happened to his Jewish workers. And what about the colored servants you had?"

Monique's voice cooled. "Half-breeds are not welcome here any more."

Louisa drew back with a sharp intake of breath. Monique knew that Harry was part Maori, descended from a race of dark-skinned people. Was that another excuse for what she had done? Louisa's eyes clouded with anger at the ignorance of the woman who stood before her. "You're no better than *them*."

She was distracted by the sudden permeating throb of machinery from the lower floor. Her heart leapt. If she wasn't mistaken, everything now made sense.

The distant sound of a dinner gong reverberated through the open door, catching her off guard.

Before she could recover, Monique kicked her aside. As Louisa staggered to regain her balance, Monique suddenly crashed to the hard floor with a shriek. Joe had grabbed her around the legs in his best imitation of a rugby tackle. She lay stunned and quiet, her eyes closed.

Louisa bent over her. "She's hit her head." A trickle of blood ran down Monique's temple. "But she's still breathing." Louisa picked up the parcel and headed through the doorway. "It's the witch's turn to be in the tower." With a satisfying click, she locked the door on Monique and turned to Joe. "She said that no one ever comes up here. With any luck, she'll never be let out."

"Mission accomplished," Joe breathed, as they worked their way swiftly down the stairs.

Louisa grimaced. "Not quite. What are you like with machinery?"

He stole a sideways glance. "Depends on what sort."

"We've a printing press to disable, Joe. Think you can do it?"

He nodded. "I'll give it a go."

Checking to see that the coast was clear, Louisa quickly followed the direction of the sound. It was behind double doors at the far end of the hall.

Signaling to Joe to follow, she readied her revolver and eased open one of the doors. Wincing at the machine's deafening clatter, she and Joe slipped into the room unnoticed.

Keeping her eye on a man working at the far end of the room, Louisa waited for Joe to perform his first act of sabotage.

Seconds ticked by.

Perspiration broke out on her brow and her heart beat swiftly against her ribs. *What was taking him so long?*

As the man glanced up, she ducked out of sight and held her breath. *Come on, Joe.*

Suddenly the room was silent, the big machine brought to a standstill.

She watched the worker hurrying to investigate. If Joe didn't get out of there, *right now*, he would be discovered...

Just as she was about to take action, Joe

appeared by her side.

But Louisa had not finished yet.

Once outside the room, she crept around to the under-stair cupboard. Opening the door, she reached in to withdraw a grenade from the ammunition box and quietly closed the door again.

Silently, they crossed to the dining room. The door was shut, but that did not completely mask the diners' voices. As Louisa withdrew the deadly object from her pocket, Joe's eyes widened.

"Open the door on the count of three," she whispered. "Two...three..." He flung the door open and she heaved the grenade into the room.

Joe grabbed her arm and they sprinted down a hallway, the sound of exploding glass crashing in their ears as they rushed out the back entrance. The kitbag thumped wildly against Louisa's back, echoing the heartbeat in her chest. Clattering down the steps, they made for a grove of trees. Louisa stumbled. Her ankle was still weak.

Joe raced ahead of her only to suddenly halt, spin around and hold out his hand to her. She clasped it as if it were a lifeline, and her feet flew almost off the ground as he tugged her along with him. The strength in his arm was like plugging into a power source, giving her the energy she needed for that final burst of speed. Safely ensconced in the shadows, Louisa sucked in gulps of air. Beside her, Joe did the same.

She glanced back at the chateau where a couple of uniformed men, dazed and bleeding, staggered onto the forecourt. Shrieking, white-aproned kitchen staff, some clutching their heads, some gesticulating wildly, ran out behind them.

Louisa glanced at Joe, unable to prevent a satisfied smile from curving her lips. "That's one piece of business they weren't expecting."

"You certainly live up to your name," he murmured.

She raised an eyebrow but he started to move ahead, hauling her with him. The distant sound of barking dogs made the hair on her neck stiffen. She glanced past Joe to where the trees merged into thick, dark shadows. Sucking in a ragged breath, she followed him into the cool darkness.

She ran as though the hounds were already snapping at her heels. She imagined she could feel their hot breath on her skin, could hear their menacing low-throated growls, could see their glowing eyes staring from behind every tree.

With the sound of blood pounding in her ears, she tried to ignore the beginnings of a painful stitch nagging at her side. She wished, too late, that she'd made more effort to take the Special Operation's cross-country fitness training more seriously. Taking shortcuts along the course had seemed a good idea at the time...

Joe was powering on and she had to strive hard to keep up with him.

As they intruded deeper into the woods, the sounds of the dogs faded. Although she knew it would be only a short respite, that the grove was sure to be searched, the exhilaration of the morning's success seemed to put wings on her feet. It was so good to have achieved something and to use her initiative, as she'd been encouraged to do. And, most satisfying of all was to have given Monique a well-deserved taste of her own medicine.

The lift in her heart at this thought matched the leap she took over the fallen log blocking the path.

Crunch!

Taken aback to find herself facedown in the dirt, she gasped for breath. Lifting her head, she spat out gritty earth and swiped a sticky leaf away with her hand.

She pulled herself to her feet. Joe had already spun around to head back toward her. She waved him on to indicate she was fine, but wasn't surprised he'd come back. It seemed second nature to him to always behave like a perfect gentleman, solicitous in his attentions.

"I'm all right," she hastily assured him. "We must keep going."

She drew comfort from the concern she saw reflected in his eyes. She could trust him implicitly. Yes, she decided, they had become good friends and friends never let one another down.

Unexpectedly, Harry's face swam into her mind.

She ground her teeth together. Even now, would she never be free of the memory, of the torture of guilt?

Putting her head down, she ran and ran until she was too exhausted to think beyond keeping her shaky, aching limbs moving.

****

Joe skidded on the sludge of slippery leaves as he slowed to a halt. Ahead of him was a clearing. Sunlight sparkled on a ribbon of water snaking its way down the valley and he heard the distant shriek of a train whistle. He doubled over as his breathing began to slow, supporting himself with a hand against a tree trunk.

Louisa drew alongside him, panting hard. She wasn't as fit as he'd expected her to be. He stole a sideways glance at her face. Perspiration beaded her forehead.

He swallowed against a rise of panic. The stakes had been well and truly raised. Where on earth could they possibly find a safe haven?

Louisa hooked an arm through his. "What do you think we should do?"

"Just keep going, I reckon." He glanced at her.

She pointed into the distance. "There's a village about five miles upstream. I know a woman there who may help us."

Joe nodded. "Come on. We've got a war to win." Catching her hand, he broke into a jog.

****

The breeze toyed with Louisa's hair until it lay in tangled ringlets. When they reached the banks of the stream she jogged alongside Joe, matching her pace to his, his hand holding hers. Her nostrils filled with the sweet scents of the meadow and the air hummed with the busy sounds of bees as the sun beat down on their heads. The peaceful country scene belied the sights and sounds of war. She wished that they could stop and enjoy it for a while.

Joe's grip was firm, her smaller hand swallowed up in his large one. She glanced at him. His face was set with concentration. He met her gaze. Just one look, but it was powerful enough to make her knees weaken.

Her coat was stifling hot. The kitbag weighed heavily on her shoulders. She knew that she had only to ask and Joe would carry it, but if she and Joe became separated, she risked losing the only item that she cared about—the pillow, her last memento of Harry.

With the back of her free hand, she brushed damp hair from her forehead. Her legs threatened to go on strike and her mouth was as dry as dust. She cast a longing look at the cool stream and yearned to paddle her swollen feet. She slowed to walking pace.

"Ankle playing up? We'll rest soon," Joe promised.

"No," Louisa groaned. "We must push on."

Joe pointed out a shelter of trees in the distance. Louisa agreed that it would be best to head under their cover for the night. They were too vulnerable out in the open.

She trudged on through the warm afternoon, lagging now behind Joe, whose longer stride placed him well ahead.

At last reaching the shade of the thicket, Louisa sank down to her knees at the stream to suck in cupped handfuls of scooped water. Then she splashed it over her hot face, not caring that it trickled down inside her blouse. Tearing her shoes and stockings off, she sighed blissfully as she dipped her toes into the current.

Joe hauled some dead branches together and formed them into a shelter. He placed bracken over the top and plumped up leaves for the floor.

"We'd best not light a fire. Too risky," he told her. Instead, as darkness came, they huddled together under the shelter for warmth. She relaxed against Joe's chest, welcoming the secure enfolding of his arms around her.

Louisa tipped her face up to look at him. "What are you thinking?" She reached to stroke the stubble grazing his chin.

He blew out his cheeks. "Too tired to think of anything except, maybe, a good, hot meal."

She laughed softly. "Men...their stomachs always take priority." She burrowed into her handbag and drew out a paper bag of peppermints.

Joe dropped a kiss on her nose. "One day I'm going to take you to a posh hotel. We'll order champagne."

Louisa sighed and offered him a mint. If only that could be possible, she thought. They both fell silent.

After a while, she said, "The Boche are always alert for anyone who looks as though they've been sleeping rough. We'll need to tidy ourselves up a bit before we hit the road." She sat up and drew out a brush from her handbag. "If I don't tackle the knots in my hair now, it'll be even worse by morning." She sighed ruefully.

Joe reached for the brush. Surprised, she raised an eyebrow. In reply, he merely gestured to her to turn her back to him. Slowly, he began to brush her hair.

"There's something I need to...*ouch*..." Louisa winced as the brush caught on a tangled knot,

"…ask."

He gentled his approach a little.

She mumbled encouragement, enjoying the rhythmic stroking. No man had ever offered to perform such an intimate task for her but then, she'd never before met a man like Joe Fisher. He was someone a girl could really fall for, if she wasn't careful.

"Joe," she said, recalling her question, "when you said that I lived up to my name, what did you mean?"

He paused in his task. "Do you not know the meaning of your Christian name?" She melted as he touched his lips to her ear. "It's a beautiful and noble one." His breath sighed against her skin. "Louisa means 'famed fighter.'"

"I'm not famous," she protested, giggling softly at the tickling on her neck.

"You're famous to me," he said, pressing hot kisses along her jaw. "My brave warrior tigress."

She opened her mouth to speak but he silenced her with a long, deep kiss. Her heart swelled, painfully, longingly.

A snuffling sound behind them made her stiffen. She jerked her mouth away. "What's that?" she whispered, staring wide-eyed into the darkened trees.

Joe raised his head, listening, neck muscles tensed. His voice low, he suggested, "Just a small animal—a hedgehog, perhaps." Then he added uncertainly, "Are there any hedgehogs in France?" He cradled her to him, felt her tremble and stroked her hair, soothing, "It's all right, my lovely. There won't be anyone searching now till dawn."

My lovely. How long had it been since anyone… She squeezed her eyes shut against the night, against the war, tightened her arms around his waist and, in an effort to control her trembling, buried her face in his chest. "What will tomorrow bring?"

His breath caught. "Who's to say what our future is?"

The thump of his beating heart pulsed against her cheek. She absorbed his scent—primitive, wild, male. Her chin lifted to seek his lips almost as of its own accord. Too exhausted to fight it, not wanting to even try, she surrendered fully to the bliss of his hot caress. Desire built, heating her sensitive inner core, agonizingly, deliciously. She squirmed against him, catching her breath as she grazed his hardened maleness.

Joe instantly stilled, and she absorbed the controlled tension of his arousal into her own restless bones. The past...the future...he was offering her a moment to forget them both.

"Show me," he whispered urgently, "that you're ready for this." His fingers stroked the line of her cheek and she nuzzled against them as delicate sparks jumped along her nerve endings. The black night wrapped itself around them like a cozy blanket, as if enclosing them in their own secret world. She reached up blindly, her fingers curling around a lock of his hair.

He tensed and Louisa sucked in a shallow breath. "This may be our only chance." She tugged him closer.

"I hope not, dear..." His warm sigh fluttered across her lips. He captured her face within his trembling, warm palms and she was lost, swirling into eternity, down ever deeper into their private, intimate abyss.

She gasped softly when he moved to press sweet, tender kisses on her cheeks and neck, sighed with joy as his lips returned to hers. His fingers searched blindly for each button, popping them open, exposing her pale skin to the air. She wasn't cold—hot liquid fanned within.

"Your skin..." Joe rasped thickly, stroking her,

"it's so soft, so smooth." She combed her fingers through his short silky hair as he nuzzled her blouse and underwear aside, and felt for each nipple with his tongue. She moaned softly as he suckled. His lips again avidly sought hers. She spanned her hands across his strong shoulders before slipping them between the sides of his unbuttoned shirt.

She smoothed her way along his chest, toyed with each nipple, rubbed her flattened palm across the raised peaks.

His breathing quickened, encouraging her to arrow down his flat belly and under the leather belt of his trousers. At his low groan, she edged her hand further down to find the curled, springy hair below.

He reached to still her hand, his fingers fumbling with the buttons. She slipped open his belt buckle.

Her hand closed around him. Delighting in the velvety, smooth softness of the skin beneath her fingers, she began a slow dance of massage along the hardened length. His tongue teased her lips. He eased away from her, reaching down to gather up her skirt. His hand slipped between her legs, caressed along the edges of her panties, stroked tantalizingly across her swollen softness.

Excited, urgently wanting him, she arched her back. He murmured, "My lovely, not long now." He turned away for a moment and she quickly peeled off her underwear.

"Yes," she breathed, reaching for him to kiss her again. As one finger pushed deep inside her, she met his tongue with hers.

"You're so very lovable." He moved to smother kisses all the way down her body. She held her breath as he met the sensitive skin of her inner thighs.

Briefly closing her eyes, she gasped at the unexpected heat of his tongue on her most intimate place. Through a crescendo of almost torturous, exquisitely delicate sensation, she heard him murmur, "You feel so beautiful..."

She readied her body to receive him. He brought his lips back to hers. She sighed against his mouth, "Now... "

He moved.

She responded.

His powerful strength surged deep. Wrapping her legs around him, she cocooned them both within the transforming heat of blissful, aching pleasure.

He lay still as their breathing slowed and she gloried in the weight of him. She felt...*safe*.

"Thank you." With passion-tender lips, he brushed her forehead. "I needed your love." In a voice thick with emotion, he added, "And I always will." He rolled away with a satisfied sigh.

Louisa listened to the steady rise and fall of his breathing, her heart heavy. How could she freely return his love when her own heart was still bound in chains?

You have a beautiful, noble name... She hugged the precious words to herself. *Famed fighter.* The recall seared her with renewed shafts of pleasure.

She sighed. Making love with him had been pure madness. They had each sought a morsel of comfort, some respite, that's all.

She drew her velvet pillow close and buried her face in its softness. *Forgive me, Harry.* A single hot tear rolled down her cheek. Shivering against the chilly air, Louisa arranged her coat to cover both Joe and herself. As he reached for her, she snuggled against him, grateful for his warmth and companionship. She shuddered at the thought of being on her own in the thickening black night.

But she couldn't avoid fearing for the future. What would await them in the village? Would they find safety or would the Boche be watching for them?

An icy quiver of apprehension snaked down her spine. Reprisals for killing German Officers were horribly severe.

Her heart sank. She'd made them both vulnerable by allowing Joe to get under her skin—and into her bed. And, as she looked up at the star-studded sky, she made up her mind.

In the morning, she would put that right.

Chapter Twelve

Joe awoke at dawn. He eased himself from under Louisa's coat before tucking it back into her side. He glanced at her face, his body hardening with renewed desire. She'd been so warm, so generous. It had happened naturally; had seemed so right. And it *was* right. Her loving, a beacon of hope in the midst of war, filled him with optimism for the future.

He took his survival kit to the stream, drank a handful of water, washed, shaved and combed his hair.

Louisa joined him as he lit up a cigarette. She washed and applied powder and cherry red lipstick, peering into a compact mirror.

"Any chance of a morning kiss?" he suggested lightly.

She turned to him with an odd, half-flirtatious, half-hesitant smile. It was cute, Joe mused, her morning-after shyness. She pressed her lips to his but, too soon for him, she eased away. He reached to fold her to him again, but she suddenly stiffened.

Without quite meeting his eyes, she said, "Joe, about last night. It can't happen again."

Shocked breathless, as if she'd punched him in the ribs, he searched her face for a long moment. Tossing his cigarette onto the ground, he said tightly, "Did it mean nothing to you?" And then he realized. She was worried perhaps, about a child. He hastened to reassure her. "You know that I used…"

"Yes, of course." She shook her head. "It's not that. Please don't be angry. I don't want to fight with you."

Desperate for her to explain and yet dreading

what he might hear, he strode away a few feet, paced back and forth and returned to her. "Lou, I'm not angry but I'm sure as hell frustrated. Dammit, we're good together! And I'm not just referring to last night, though that was the most passionate—"

"No...please..." Blushing furiously, she glanced away.

Hell! She regretted their liaison! Joe's heart hammered and his arm muscles twitched as though preparing to fight. He wanted to shake her, he wanted to kiss her, he wanted to slap her, he wanted to...He swallowed down the frightening, choking dryness in his throat. He needed to hug her so fiercely to him that she'd absorb into her very pores how sincerely he felt, so that she'd know how much...just how much he cared. He wanted to do that so badly, yet his arms remained stubbornly rigid, held against his sides as though he was back on parade, standing to attention. What could he say, what could he do? A dull ache in the pit of his belly gnawed at him.

She lifted a trembling hand to shade her eyes. He bit his lower lip as the lump in his throat swelled. What was she struggling with? Fear that the war could part them at any moment? Was that what drove her to dash his dreams?

Perhaps he was being impatient. Softening his voice, he began, "Maybe later..."

She lifted her chin. "Later?" Her gaze met his.

"After all this is over. The war, I mean."

Louisa's shoulders slumped. "I don't know, Joe. Nothing ever stays the same."

The dull sadness in her voice made him ache to banish it, to tell her that he understood. But, the truth was, he couldn't comprehend just what she was so afraid of. It seemed so unlike her. Confused, but determined to break her stubborn stance, he folded his arms across his chest. "There's something you're not telling me."

A twig snapped and Louisa whipped around, her revolver already in her hand. They both stilled instantly, eyes wide.

Joe felt for his gun. His heart was rapping so hard he thought it would burst out of his chest. He held his breath and waited. He could see no movement, no sign of anyone.

After a moment, Louisa quietly heaved up her kitbag.

Joe caught her eye and, hugging the parcel to his chest, he gestured for her to follow as he began to tread a careful path out of the woods. They trudged, without speaking, as lightly as they could along the forest floor.

But Joe was adamant that all his hopes would not be destroyed. He needed to know the whole truth—he swallowed at the thought of the unpalatable consequences—no matter how hurtful the facts were. As soon as they'd slipped deeper into the camouflage of the forest, he said, "You're right. One of us could be killed at any moment." He glanced at her, grimly. "But I'm damned if I'll rest in peace knowing that I've merely been used by you." He twisted his lips ruefully. "You don't care for me at all, do you!"

She blanched and rounded on him, eyes glittering. Her mouth opened then closed as if she'd thought better of it.

She really doesn't care for me. His heart plunged in savage disappointment and he stumbled over a hidden root. Struggling with pride, he immediately widened his stride to distance himself.

"Joe!" Louisa caught up to him. "All right!" She plucked her lip. "It's probably only fair that you know everything."

Joe didn't slacken his pace and kept his eyes focused on the way ahead. Why had she suddenly changed her mind? "Up to you," he said tightly.

"I've never told anyone else this." Louisa

touched his shoulder. "But maybe it'll help you understand."

At last, a chink in her armor. *Now we're getting somewhere.* He gave her a cautious glance.

"He...Harry..." Louisa took a deep breath, "was attacked because Monique had sent us to a false rendezvous. We were to deliver leaflets which had been printed at the newspaper office where we worked. The...leaflets contained an article critical of the occupation."

Joe sucked in his bottom lip. "Dangerous."

"Yes. But it was an attempt to tell the truth, to alert the public to what was happening."

"Surely he realized the risk he was taking?"

"No, he didn't have any idea."

Joe frowned. "What do you mean?" He couldn't believe that anyone would be that stupid.

"I mean," Louisa said shakily, "that he walked into a trap because he didn't write it."

Joe stared at her, incredulous. "You're saying that he was framed by Monique? But...*why?*" Dodging a low tree branch, he paused to hold it back for her, adding, "Do you know who the real author was?"

She held his gaze. "It was me."

His jaw dropped. He didn't know what to say.

She hurriedly elaborated, "You have to understand that he was a journalist based in Paris. I was a sub-editor but I became increasingly frustrated that we were so restricted in what could be reported." She halted and turned to Joe, pain etched on her face. "I saw them beating him..." Her voice rose. "And I couldn't do anything about it. I couldn't stop them! Joe, oh God..." Her eyes beseeched him as she whispered, "It should have been me."

Joe's gut twisted at the anguish in her voice. In an effort to comfort, he reached out for her.

"No." She held up both hands and took a step

backward. "You presume I'm brave—"

"And you are," he insisted. "You volunteered for a tough training course, threw yourself out of a plane in the dead of night, blew a bunch of Jerry to smithereens—"

"No," she interrupted, "No!" Stricken with guilt and shame, she whispered, "I'm a coward."

"Don't be so hard on yourself!"

Choking back tears, she croaked, "I should have told them the truth and given myself up. They might have released him."

Joe, sickened at the idea that she could have exposed herself to the possibility of a beating or worse, said harshly, "They wouldn't have listened, you know that! Men like that aren't interested in the facts. It was blood they were after—both of you would have been sacrificed!" He offered her his handkerchief. As her trembling fingers accepted it, a wave of compassion calmed his anger. Gentling his tone, he said, "I've heard it said that the enemy within us is the toughest foe." He bent his knees to gaze into her face. "I wasn't sure what that meant—till now." He caught her hand. "Don't let guilt over his death destroy us."

A bird swooped down in front of them. Louisa blinked, startled, and with a bleakness that caught at Joe's heart, she grated, "Dealing with Monique hasn't made me feel any better about what I did to Harry." A flash of despair lit her eyes.

He straightened up and wiped his hands slowly down his face. To Joe the answer was clear—but Louisa was too emotionally involved to see it. She wouldn't like it, but he knew he had to say it, anyway. It was the only way he could think of to help her get through this private hell.

He drew in a breath. "Perhaps it's because you've never really let him go. Isn't it time you said goodbye?"

"I can't."

"Can't?" he challenged, glancing at the stubborn set of her mouth. "Or won't?"

She flinched. He'd gone too far. Raising her chin, she looked him in the eye. "You should get back to England as soon as you can. Once you're flying again, you'll forget all about me."

Without another word, she turned on her heel and left him to follow her.

Joe lagged behind, his chest tightening in frustration. He knew what he *should* do. He should do as she said, save his own skin, leave her alone, do what she declared she wanted him to do. He didn't need reminding of his duty toward rejoining his squadron.

She thought it would be easy to forget her? He squared his shoulders. No, if she thought that he was just going to give in, then all he could say was: *Not on your Nelly*.

He broke into a trot to catch up with her. She kept her face stubbornly averted but he wasn't put off. "Bloody hell, I may try to forget you, but before I leave France, I'm going to make damn sure that you'll always remember *me!*"

She hadn't expected that. Catching her as she stumbled, he had the wry satisfaction—for the second time since they'd met—of seeing Louisa's jaw drop.

****

Louisa clutched at the gripping hunger pains in her stomach. What she wouldn't give for a taste of *pain au chocolat* right now. The very thought of it made her feel faint.

Joe drew up beside her as she stopped to survey the landscape. She could see the village she was heading for, and to her relief it was only a short distance away. She cocked an ear to listen for sounds of enemy activity. It was early morning and all she heard was the soft sigh of a gathering breeze rustling the long grass.

As they reached the main street, she noted it appeared to be deserted. But caution directed her to say, "We'll take the back roads."

After carefully retracing her route, she approached the cream-plastered house where a gnarled wisteria trailed along the walls, praying she had remembered the correct address.

She lifted the wrought iron knocker on the faded blue door. The noise echoed down the quiet street. No answer. She glanced at Joe but he avoided meeting her eye.

A white cat jumped down from a nearby wall. Startled, Louisa took a deep breath to steady herself.

The cat entwined itself around Joe's legs, meowing loudly.

"You're hungry too, eh?" Joe bent to tickle under the cat's chin.

A woman in the next house opened her door. A frown formed on her face as she stared at them.

Louisa, anxious to allay suspicion, smiled and said, "Bonjour Madame." The woman returned her greeting and started to sweep the front step.

Louisa knocked once more. This time she was rewarded when the door swung back. Louisa, fingers crossed, gave the password.

Madame Kleber welcomed Louisa and Joe into her dark hallway with a huge smile and her arms flung wide. The tantalizing smell of food sizzling on the hob wafted around them. Louisa sank gratefully into the offered chair.

Later, while indulging in the luxury of a hot bath, she allowed a moment to think of Joe. She slid the soap over her wet skin and closed her eyes. She imagined Joe's hands exploring her, his lips, his body, his loving—exquisitely ardent and yet so tender—and squirmed helplessly against her shivers of excitement.

She arched her head back under the water to rinse her hair. Wash away these thoughts of Joe, she told herself. She was well aware her rejection had offended him but she knew it was for the best. It was over and done with.

She grabbed a towel and rubbed her hair so hard that it was as if she was trying to exorcise a demon. But no amount of physical effort could erase the realization that Joe meant much more to her than merely a one-night dalliance. *Merde.*

****

"A letter came for you." Madame Kleber handed Louisa an envelope. In answer to Louisa's questioning look she said, "It was delivered yesterday."

Louisa tore it open. There could be only one person who would know where to contact her.

As she'd expected, it was from Dickie. She read: *I hope that you'll receive this information. I tried to tell you as you left on the train. Claude was in Monique's pay. He was supplying information to her in exchange for the payment of his debts at the brothel.*

Louisa allowed herself a grim smile of satisfaction. So she had been right about Claude. It explained why he was so keen to get his hands on the Resistance money. No doubt he saw it as a means to buy himself out of Monique's manipulative control.

She read on. *Monique was about to expose you in the café. KEEP AWAY FROM HER.* Louisa grimaced. Too late for that. *P.S. The dice are on the table.*

The last sentence was obviously in code.

Destroying the note immediately, Louisa dried her hair in a patch of sun from the window and made a start on deciphering the words she'd committed to memory.

She was interrupted by Madame Kleber bustling past in response to a knock at the door. As the door closed, Louisa glanced up to see her broad face pale, her eyes dilated.

"My neighbour... she warns me ze Boche are searching each house in ze street!" Madame Kleber crossed the room to a small font suspended in an alcove on a wall, dipped a finger and crossed herself with holy water.

Even as her heart sank, an idea occurred to Louisa. "Do you have an attic?"

"Oui."

"Show me, s'il vous plait."

Louisa stowed the kitbag there. By the time she had completed this task, Joe was out of the bath. He wandered into the room and her heart lurched at the sight of his scrubbed-up appearance. She inhaled his freshly clean scent and admired the way that wisps of black hair curled damply against his neck.

But when she caught his eye, she blushed at his cool stare. He'd plainly decided to take her at her word, emotionally distancing himself in preparation for when they'd have to part physically. She quashed a stab of remorse, reminding herself that it was what she'd wanted. *Good,* she thought defiantly. His coldness was making it easier for her.

Her eyes fell on the parcel that Joe had casually dropped in the corner. Maybe now would be the right time to reveal its contents.

"What's wrong?" Joe's brows drew together in a frown.

She told him. "There's no point in us running. We won't get far. There are too many troops about."

She shook out the nun's habit in front of him. "I want you to wear this. You must pretend that you have taken a vow of silence."

The look on Joe's face was as if she'd asked him to cut off his manhood. "That's what I've been carrying around all this time?"

"It'll match your footwear," she teased.

Joe shot her a withering glance.

Louisa sighed. "Don't argue—just put it on."

"I've got a better idea." Joe thrust the offending garment under her nose. "You wear it. It'll match your martyrdom."

That was below the belt. Her bile rose. "I'm not the one who can't speak a word of French or German!" Louisa snatched a breath before adding, in a placatory tone, "Joe, we haven't got time for this."

Madame Kleber, peering through the window, suddenly pulled away, flapping her hands. Beads of perspiration had formed on her upper lip and her face was contorted in fear.

"Zey are almost here." Her voice came out in a nervous squeak.

Louisa bounded up the stairs and ran to the attic ladder, with Joe hot on her heels. Both of them scaled it quickly, hauling up the ladder behind them.

Joe carefully placed the cover over, blocking out every pinprick of light from the landing below.

Louisa crouched in the stuffy, black darkness, listening to the blood pounding in her ears. Beside her, she sensed the rapid rise and fall of Joe's chest.

She heard a rustling sound. No doubt they had disturbed a mouse, or worse, a rat. Maybe a whole nest of them. A shiver ran through her. She reached to clutch Joe's arm, then thought she'd better not.

She willed herself to concentrate on listening to the goings-on below. If the Boche interpreted Madame Kleber's signs of panic as indications of guilt, then she and Joe would be in deep, deep trouble.

Loud banging on the door reverberated throughout the house. Louisa tensed as Joe held his breath.

The muffled sounds of clipped guttural voices, alternating with Madame's mellow tone, floated through the edges of the trapdoor. Louisa discovered that her eyes had adjusted to the darkness. She found herself staring at a narrow shaft of light beaming through the roof. When her gaze followed it to its source, she observed what looked like another opening.

Heavy footsteps thundered up the stairs. Louisa's chest tightened painfully as the sounds passed directly beneath them and immediately onward to the bedrooms.

"Vot is here?" The sudden sharp voice below sent a jolt of adrenaline coursing through her veins.

She whispered in Joe's ear, "There's a hatch onto the roof. I'll try to open it."

Lowering herself onto all fours, Louisa crawled slowly along the beams, conscious of the fact that one slip could send her crashing through the ceiling and down to the searchers' waiting arms. Perspiration prickled uncomfortably under her clothing.

She reached the hatch. Her arms stretched. Her fingers pushed.

It didn't budge.

She groped around and found a small rope attached. She pulled it as hard as she could.

It stayed stuck.

Something scraped across the under-side of the ceiling trapdoor. The attic was about to be searched.

Louisa used all her strength in an effort to shift the hatch but it still remained fast. She could hear Joe right behind her. He reached up with both hands and pushed hard. Daylight streamed through, in blinding volume, as the hatch silently opened outwards and lay flat against the roof.

Louisa stood up. Her upper body was through. Bracing her arms on either side of the opening she dragged her lower half up onto the tiles.

Turning back she watched Joe do the same, closing the hatch behind him.

From the roof, Louisa could see for miles around but she wasn't inclined to enjoy the view. With her back wedged firmly against the chimney, she drew in deep breaths. Her pulse rate was over the scale and her limbs were like jelly.

Keeping her eye on the roof hatch, she listened for sounds of movement. Suddenly it occurred to her that she could block the hatch being opened, by leaning her weight on it. Inching her way carefully over, she proceeded to do just that.

It was then that she noticed that Joe was lying face down against the steep, tiled slope. His arms were spread-eagled as if clinging on to avoid a slip.

A shout from the street—orders were being given for the soldiers to move on to the next house.

With curiosity nudging her to confirm what she was hearing, she moved closer to the edge and peered over.

"Joe," she whispered loudly. "Looks like they're leaving..." The words died on her lips as, out of the corner of her eye, she saw the lid of the hatch slowly rise.

Chapter Thirteen

Louisa twisted around and flattened herself against the slope of the roof. She stretched to clamp down the lid but was too late as with a dull oomph, it was flung back and a young girl's head appeared in the opening.

"Bonjour, Madamoiselle," the girl said shyly. "My mama says you must not return to ze house. Guards are posted on ze street."

"You are Madame Kleber's daughter?"

"Oui." The girl nodded. "Sabine." She held out a package to Louisa. "She said to give you zis."

"What is it?"

"Some food, I zink, and a few francs. Zat's all she could spare."

"Merci, Sabine." Louisa took the offering. "And thank your mother for us."

Sabine started to withdraw but, as she did so, Louisa remembered something. "Just a moment! My bag—will you fetch it for me, s'il vous plait?"

Sabine's head disappeared, popping up a minute later. She heaved the kitbag up over the lip of the opening and slid it towards Louisa's waiting hand.

"Good girl, Sabine. Just one more thing—we'll need some rope. Can you help?"

"I will see. Wait here."

Louisa smiled grimly at that. It wasn't as though she and Joe had any other choice. She glanced his way. He was still in exactly the same position that he'd been in before. Something wasn't right. "Joe," she murmured. "Try to edge over towards me."

Joe groaned. His breathing was rapid and

perspiration trickled down his forehead.

"What's wrong?" She frowned. Was he ill?

Joe rolled to one side, revealing damp patches of sweat on the front of his clothes. A shiver ran through him, but as if he guessed what she was thinking, he muttered, "I'm not ill."

Suddenly, Louisa understood. But how the heck did a pilot, she immediately wondered, come to have a problem with heights? *Merde!*

Just then, Sabine returned with the rope. "I hope it is long enough."

Gritting his teeth, Joe reached up and grasped the line. "Let's get this over and done with."

Louisa, quickly securing the line around the chimney, abseiled down the slope of the roof and onto a flat area next door. She tugged on the line to indicate that Joe should follow.

Seconds passed.

She looked up. He hadn't moved from where she'd left him. His back was turned towards her, she couldn't see his face, but she could feel the line quivering between her hands.

She tugged the rope again, more firmly this time and heard him answer with another groan. "I can't do it."

A bullet slammed into the chimney, pinging shards of mortar towards Louisa. She ducked.

Joe called softly, his voice urgent, "Lou! Be careful!"

Shame inflamed her cheeks. She'd led Joe into this situation. She was grateful for all his help, but now... She glanced up. Now he was petrified, trapped by a crippling phobia. And yet, in spite of what she'd said to him earlier in the day, his concern was all for her.

"There's the fraulein!" A shout from below.

Fraulein? Could it be that they were only searching for *her*? Relief flooded Louisa. If this was true, and she prayed that it was, then Joe had a chance to be overlooked.

Instantly, decision made, she dropped the line and jumped off the edge of the roof, tumbling out-of-sight into the garden below.

****

Hearing the shout, Joe forced himself to glance down. His heart dropped as he saw Louisa's deliberate leap. What the hell was she doing?

More excited shouts, climbing in volume. Joe's belly clenched with fear. Was she hurt? She'd be waiting for him. Every moment he delayed was another moment that put her in danger.

Gritting his teeth, he forced himself to edge down the roof. *Must hurry.* He eased his grip on the rope, allowing it to slide more quickly through his fingers. He cursed as his shoes skittered noisily across the tiles. Desperately, he tried to find a foothold. But he'd lost control. With a stomach-lurching moan of agony, he landed heavily onto the flat part of the roof.

****

A volley of shots rang out, ricocheting loudly across the tiles. Louisa couldn't see what was happening as her view of the street was blocked by a dividing wall.

Holding a breath, her pulse beating hard, she readied her revolver and stepped sideways behind a tall conifer. As the sound of heavy-footed boots approached, she parted a stiff branch, aimed and fired.

She didn't wait to see the results. Spinning around, she thrust herself through a gap in the hedge behind her and sprinted down the narrow lane.

Just as she reached the rough stone wall at the end, a further shot cracked harshly across the roof. She heard a grunt of pain. Joe had been hit. *Merde!*

Louisa turned and retraced her steps. A high-booted leg appeared through the hedge. She fired, barely registering the enraged curse as she frantically sought an alternative route back to Joe.

Heaving herself onto the top of the wall, she glanced quickly around. Joe was prone, deathly still. She dragged off her kitbag and tossed it over, then leaped after it, landing with a heavy thump beside him.

Joe's face was ashen, his breathing shallow. A sticky, red patch was rapidly soaking into his hair.

She parted the matted strands and examined the bloodied area. She could see no entry hole, the bullet must have only grazed the flesh. Louisa fumbled for her bag and pulled out two bandages. Folding one into a pad, she pressed it onto the patch to stem the bleeding. Then she deftly wrapped the other bandage around his head to hold it in place.

"Not as bad as it looks—just a surface wound, I think." But her words fell on deaf ears. Joe had fainted.

Louisa placed two fingers on his wrist. Reassured that his pulse was strong, she took the time to make a short reconnaissance. She couldn't spot any snipers but that didn't mean that they weren't still lurking in the area.

She glanced back at Joe. Blood seeped rapidly into the bandage and trickled down his cheek. He lay awkwardly, so she tried, unsuccessfully, to move him.

Joe moaned softly. The bandage was already stained bright red.

Louisa tugged the little pillow from her kitbag and stroked her cheek with the soft, luxurious velvet. She burrowed her nose to breathe in the familiar scent. Then, briskly staunching a pang of grief, she bound it firmly against Joe's head.

As drops of blood pierced the fabric, the heavy stone in her heart grew restless. Her eyelids fluttered closed and she drew in a deep, calming breath.

But the stone could no longer be placated. It demanded to be released from its prison. So, with a wrenching sigh of anguish, Louisa bid adieu—to Harry. *Rest in peace.*

A sudden shout sent her pulse leaping. Placing her hand lightly on Joe's chest, she fanned her fingers over his beating heart. "We have to get to the ground, Joe. Do you think you can make it?"

His answer was another low moan of pain. But then he gripped her hands tightly and struggled to sit up. She pulled him towards her and together they shuffled over to the edge.

Louisa glanced down. It wasn't a very long drop and she judged that Joe should be able to make it. The grass would soften his landing.

She listened for sounds of movement below but all seemed clear. It would take time for the rest of the soldiers to find them—she hoped she had a few minutes at least. Frustrated that the high roofline prevented her being able to see to the street, she reminded herself that if she couldn't see, then neither could she and Joe be seen.

Together, they launched themselves onto the grass. They both sank to their knees, toppling forwards as they lost balance.

Joe's bandage went awry and the pillow dislodged. Louisa helped Joe to his feet, half-dragged him over to a garden shed and propped him against the wall. His breathing was labored, his lips tinged blue. Louisa adjusted his bandage with fumbling fingers, her ears alert for danger.

"Wait here, Joe. I'm going to get help."

"I'm... not... going... anywhere," he slurred.

Pressing one hand against the surge of fear that welled up in the pit of her stomach, Louisa bent to kiss his forehead. "I won't be long, I promise."

Slapping the grass seeds off her clothes, she slipped off her kitbag and stepped out of the shed, revolver in hand and eyes peeled for any threat. She ran across to a tree, waited there for a second, then ran to the back door of the house and knocked. She prayed that she had made the right choice.

The door opened to reveal the neighbor they'd both seen earlier. Would she help?

Louisa hadn't even greeted her before the door was shut firmly in her face. *Merde!*

Unwilling to risk exposing herself on the street, she struggled to think of how she could safely get an SOS to Madame Kleber. Anxiety for Joe was scrambling her mental sharpness to a tangled, emotional mess. She had a chance to do something for him, and she must not let him down.

With this thought uppermost, she glanced back to where she had left him.

She drew in a sharp breath. He was totally slumped over as if he...

She ran back towards the shed, stumbling over the uneven ground in her haste, her breath catching painfully in her throat.

Behind her, she heard a door opening. Had the woman had a change of heart? Louisa, without stopping, glanced over her shoulder. Two soldiers ran towards her. *Merde.* She must distract them away from Joe. She whirled around and ran back towards the gap in the hedge but just as she was about to push through, the men caught up with her.

As they swiftly began to march her away, she pleaded silently that a message would get through to Dickie. Joe needed urgent medical attention.

As Louisa was forced towards a waiting vehicle, she twisted and struggled in a desperate attempt to free herself.

The men cursed her and tightened their grip.

Deep in her heart she knew that it was hopeless, that she would probably never see Joe again. His hesitation on the roof had probably cost him his life.

****

Joe felt light as air. He was whirling and

spinning as though he was a dandelion seed being tossed about by a fickle wind. He was soaring high, floating up and up into a brilliant white light as sharp as diamonds.

Then, inexplicably, he was as heavy as a sack of spuds. The weight dragged him down, forcing him against the hard, unyielding ground. His head ached with the pressure of something pushing firmly, relentlessly, against it.

He opened one eye, bewildered by the overwhelming sensations. He gagged at the stink assaulting his nostrils. It was of blood and rotting leaves.

He remembered now that he was in a garden shed. His gaze traveled slowly over the pieces of gardening equipment hanging on the walls, the stacks of empty pots and a large metal watering can on the bench.

He flicked his tongue over parched lips and wondered if there was any water in that can. He stretched towards it, immediately wincing at the pain that cut through his head.

Gingerly, he touched the protruding bandage. It was damp and sticky. Withdrawing his hand, he grimaced at the crimson blood on his fingers.

Louisa had said that she wouldn't be long. He looked at his watch. It was mid-afternoon. She'd been gone for hours.

His gaze rested on her kitbag. Strange that she had left it behind. He carefully reached for it and pulled it towards him. He undid the flaps and opened it. The sweet lavender scent of her clothes immediately flooded his senses. Where was she? Was she safe?

He wanted her beside him. He was stuck in this shed with no idea of when she would return.

Knowing that she had probably risked her own safety trying to get medical aid for him, Joe's belly knotted in sickening despair. With a groan of frustration, he tried to heave himself up from the floor. But as a wave of dizziness overtook him, he fell back, his eyes closed.

Strong hands were lifting him. Pipe tobacco pervaded the air. He struggled to open his eyes but exhaustion defeated his feeble attempt.

"What's this, old chap?" Someone tugged Joe's bandage.

He tried to answer but his tongue was swollen and as dry as old hay.

"By Jove...!" Dickie sounded incredulous. "Never thought I'd see the day that Lulu would sacrifice this pillow." He lowered his voice. "It was Harry's very last gift to her."

Joe moaned as a firmer tug sent pains shooting through his skull. And then everything, mercifully, went black.

****

Louisa strained at the cords binding her wrists to the door handle of the backseat. She glanced at the driver to see if his mirror was angled towards her. It was and, *dammit*, he was keeping a close eye on her. But at least there was no one else in the vehicle—the other soldier had been dropped off in the village centre.

She refused to end up in the clutches of the Gestapo. She decided on a plan.

Laying her head on her hands, she began to weep. As she did so, she pulled at the knot with her teeth, praying that the angle of her head would disguise her actions. She shook her head in imitation of a dog worrying a bone, allowing her thick hair to fall around her face to enhance the deception. She sobbed louder, genuine tears coming easily as she thought of Joe and, all the while, her teeth worked away at the loosening of the cords.

The driver was shouting at her now but she ignored him. Increasing the volume of her wailing, she gave a final tug and felt a satisfying slackness as the cords pulled free.

She glanced up at the mirror to meet the scowling, disapproving glare of the driver. She sniffed loudly, keeping her face turned towards him to reinforce his view of her tear-stained face. But her eyes were watching the road.

The man gunned the accelerator. Louisa strained, desperate to keep her hands in a tightly-tied pose on the handle.

A sharp swerve around a corner forced her head against the door. As the driver slammed on the brakes, she slipped her hands free, grabbed the handle and tumbled out through the open door. She landed facedown in the dusty, long grass of the verge. Winded, she lay still for a second before flipping herself sideways and rolling into a deep ditch. Hastily scrambling to her feet, she cleared the ditch and ran.

A crackle of gunfire erupted from the road along with furious cursing from the driver. She was defenseless, her revolver had been confiscated, but knew she had a good head start. This gave her a spurt of confidence. She just had to keep on putting one foot in front of the other, not slacken the pace, nor give in to muscles screaming in protest.

The battering she'd taken upon landing on the verge was making its effects felt. She ached all over.

It was a long way back to the village but she couldn't afford to stop and rest. Breathing hard, she made her way to a bridge she'd noticed ahead.

Creeping under one of the shadowy stone arches, she eased herself down onto the cool riverbank.

She heard the ominous rumbling of a motor approaching the bridge. She tensed.

A floating log caught her eye. She looked more closely and sucked in a breath. It was a body—of a young woman.

Louisa stretched out, clutched the fabric of the

dress and pulled her to the bank. It was still fresh; she looked as though she were merely sleeping. Her hair, covered by a headscarf, was the same color and length as Louisa's. Louisa briefly wondered how the poor woman had met her fate.

The vehicle slowed.

Louisa acted quickly. "You haven't died in vain," she whispered, as she deftly stripped off the clothing.

The slamming of a door, swiftly followed by a shout and a gunshot, was exactly the diversion that she had hoped for. She watched her own skirt and blouse sink into the depths, dragged under by the weight of the body, then opened the leather wallet containing the woman's papers. As she heard the vehicle recede, she emerged, shivering, from under the bridge as Francoise Gerard, a farmer's wife.

Chapter Fourteen

Louisa shone a grateful smile on the farmhand as his horse and cart trundled to a stop. The breeze fluttered the sun-dried hem of her borrowed floral dress. She smoothed the bright scarf over her hair and steeled herself to face the checkpoint now in place at the edge of the village.

She placed her new papers for inspection into the outstretched hand of one of the guards.

Willing herself to relax, she tried to breathe in a normal, regular rhythm. She was Madame Gerard. If he asked her business, she would say that it was her shopping day. She just hoped he wouldn't notice she wasn't carrying a basket.

The guard frowned. "Why are your papers wet?"

Louisa had anticipated this and was ready with an explanation. "They fell out of my pocket, sir, when I was feeding the ducks in the river." She dropped her gaze.

"You shouldn't be so careless!" The guard waggled an admonishing finger as he handed her back the papers.

She fixed what she hoped was a suitably contrite expression on her face, thinking: *Bastard.* All the same, she had to admit that it had served her purpose well to pose as a frivolous girl.

"You may pass," he said, indicating for her to move forward.

There were very few people out on the street. Most would still be cowering behind closed doors, she thought. She could almost smell the fear as she hurried along the cobbled pavements.

Heart in her mouth, not sure of what she would

find, she approached the shed where she'd left Joe. She knew she should prepare for the worst.

She pushed open the creaky door and, peering into the gloom, waited for her eyes to adjust.

Empty.

She stepped in, her pulse rate climbing. Had they taken him?

Louisa knelt to pick up the discarded pillow, grimacing at the stench. It was stiff with caked, dried blood.

He'd died and they'd dragged him away.

A great sob of remorse rose from the depths of her soul—she hadn't told Joe that she loved him. And now it was too late. He'd thought she hadn't cared for him. A yawning pit opened up in her stomach. He'd died lonely, afraid and in pain and it was *all her fault.*

Wretched with regret, eyes shut and keening softly to herself, Louisa didn't hear the sound of footsteps coming up behind her nor see the approaching shadow of a figure.

"Mademoiselle?"

She whirled around at the familiar childish voice.

"*Mon dieu*...Sabine?" She laid a hand against her heart. "Do you know..." she swallowed painfully, "what happened...to my... companion?"

"Another man came and took him away, Mademoiselle."

Louisa squeezed her eyes shut as a dull weight settled in her chest. It was exactly as she'd feared.

"Mademoiselle?" Louisa felt a tap on her shoulder. "He left you zis."

Louisa groaned against the pillow, loath to open her eyes. She just wanted to be alone.

"He said zat you'd need it."

Why would the Boche say that? Was she mistaken in presuming that Joe had been taken by them? Louisa opened her eyes and sighed in relief as

Sabine indicated the kitbag.

Her pulse danced with hope. "Who took Joe? Was he all right? Sabine, it wasn't the Boche, was it?"

Sabine shook her head and shyly twirled one of her plaits between her fingers. "It was a man wiz a moustache like a hairy caterpillar who helped ze wounded foreigner."

Louisa, hiding her smile at the child's apt description of Dickie, gathered her into a joyous hug.

A deep rumbling echoed up the valley. It grew louder and the ground began to shake beneath their feet like an earthquake.

Sabine pulled away, her eyes wide with fright. "I must go to mama!" She turned, immediately bumping into the man looming in the doorway.

"What's the rush?" Dickie laughed, glancing over her head at Louisa. Sabine quickly skirted around him and loped away like a hunted gazelle.

"Darling! You all right?" he asked, as Louisa smiled a greeting.

At her affirming nod, Dickie gazed skyward as the sound of low-flying planes added to the general noise echoing around them. As the first plane swooped across, he bent an arm in a solemn salute.

"They're ours?" Louisa gasped, hardly daring to believe that the Allies had arrived. She gave Dickie an appraising glance. "You don't seem surprised."

Dickie grinned. "Didn't you receive my note?" He prompted, "Dice on the table?"

"Is that what it meant? I'm afraid I didn't get to finish decoding it."

He tucked her hand under his arm and together they made their way to the street. The curbs had rapidly filled with people, cheering and whistling, welcoming the allied tanks and trucks as they rolled on past.

Louisa licked dry lips. "How's Joe?"

"Tough as old boots," he joked. "Getting spoiled

rotten by Madame Kleber."

Her heart leapt. "I must see him."

She urged Dickie on, but as the last of the vehicles rolled on through, the excited, joyous throng swept them both out into the road. The noise was overwhelming. Singing broke out and suddenly it seemed that everyone, old and young alike, was dancing.

Dickie took Louisa into his arms. She tried to pull away, desperate to see Joe. Dickie swung her off her feet, clumsily jostling for position as they were absorbed into the crowd. Everyone was jubilant. Laughing, smiling expressions transformed the hungry, war-weary faces. People were hugging and kissing with gusto, as if they'd only just discovered the warmth of humanity.

Dickie swapped glances with Louisa as someone tapped on his shoulder. Indicating that she didn't recognize who it was, Louisa shook her head.

The tapping turned into a punch.

Scowling irritably, Dickie swung around.

A man, his teeth shining through a wildly sprouting beard and moustache, greeted him roughly. Before Dickie could reply, the man directed a vitriolic tirade at Louisa.

She shook her head in strident denial at his insistence that he knew her. When she tried to prevent the man from plucking at her clothes, Dickie began to shepherd her away.

But he pulled up short as Louisa was suddenly snatched away from him. She bucked frantically against the man's restraint, screaming at him to release her.

****

Joe, lounging in Madame Kleber's doorway, heard a shout and saw Dickie running towards him. But his wave of greeting faltered as he saw the anxiety in Dickie's expression.

"Lulu's in trouble!"

Joe blanched. "She's here? Where?" He glanced over the crowd.

"Snatched by some scruffy chap...claims she's his wife. Must have been hitting the wine a little too much—"

"We've got to go after her!" Joe steadied himself against the door frame.

"You're in no fit state to do that."

Joe ground his teeth against the aching throb in his temple. "I'll not rest until I find her, dammit. Which way did they go?" Hugely relieved to know that she wasn't incarcerated in some stinking Gestapo cell, he ignored Dickie's cries of, "Don't be a fool, man," and forcefully elbowed his way through the crowd.

Suddenly, it was as if a cold hand had clutched at his chest. He'd spotted her, along with the male, in the center of a group. Louisa was plainly frightened. Joe saw a woman point to her.

It was Monique! His heart dropped as the Frenchwoman's shouting set off a reaction amongst the bystanders. Joe couldn't understand what was being said, but one glance at their menacing gestures and jeering and booing made him sick with horror.

As he drew closer, he could see that Louisa was trying to give the bloke something. Was she attempting to bribe him? The man released her and began to examine the wallet of papers.

An enraged cry went up from the crowd. Joe bit his lip as Louisa was hustled and shoved by the excited group of hecklers.

Dickie caught up to him. "They think she's a collaborator! They're saying she slept with the enemy."

"What will they do to her?"

"They'll rough her up. Maybe even..." Dickie swallowed, unable to finish.

"Lynch her? Is that what you're trying to say?"

One look at his face confirmed Joe's fears. He knew he had no chance of getting Louisa out of this mess without Dickie's help and pulled him aside. "Did you hear Monique?" At Dickie's affirmative scowl, Joe said, "I have an idea."

He hurried Dickie back to Madame Kleber's and quickly found what he was looking for—the nun's habit should just do the trick.

At Dickie's incredulous glance, Joe said, "I'm going to mingle with the crowd. When I shoot a few rounds in the air, that'll be your cue to grab Louisa."

"They'll never expect a nun to behave like that!" Dickie scoffed.

Joe raised his eyebrows. "Exactly."

They could hear the crowd getting louder. Heart in his mouth, Joe signaled to Dickie and stepped outside. He scanned the crowd for Monique and silently made his way towards her.

The crowd parted to allow the nun through and, belatedly, he silently thanked Louisa for her foresight in acquiring the disguise. And he'd given her a hard time about it...

He glanced up to see Monique almost right in front. He cringed back—had she seen him? But she ignored the nun. Her eyes were focused somewhere else. He followed her glare and his heart plummeted.

Louisa was only a few yards ahead. He sucked in a breath as Monique aimed her revolver.

Joe raised his arm, knocked the gun away, heaved her over his shoulder and sprinted towards Louisa, spraying the air with bullets.

He just had time to register the astonished look on Louisa's face before Dickie snatched her away. Together, they all dashed to the house and Joe collapsed, breathing hard, inside the sanctuary of Madame Kleber's hallway.

Enraged shouts and frenzied banging on the other side of the bolted door sent shivers of ice down Joe's spine.

As Madame Kleber fussily ushered them towards the living room, Monique, with a cry of fury, lunged at Louisa. This time, Joe didn't hesitate to shoot her.

Monique crumpled to the floor and Louisa reached for Joe.

"*Mon Dieu!*" she breathed. "You really are alive!"

He gave a dry laugh. "Yes, thanks to you." He glanced toward Dickie. "I know what that cushion meant to you." In a low voice, he added reverently, "It saved my life."

The words squeezed her heart. She squinted up at him, tears stinging behind her eyes.

Joe glanced, with a wry grimace, to where Monique's body lay. "She was intent on destroying you, one way or another. I shouldn't have interfered with your plans for her at the chateau."

"It doesn't matter!" Relief buckled her knees and she fell gratefully into his arms. "All I care about is that you're safe." She heaved a huge sigh.

He stroked her hair and murmured, "And now that I know that you're all right," he crushed her closer, "you'll be pleased that tonight I'm away to England."

Suddenly, Louisa's joy deflated like a popped balloon as she inwardly sagged with disbelief. He was leaving? Just when she'd discovered the depth of her feelings?

"Monique..."

She flinched at the catch in Dickie's voice and turned to see him gazing at his ex-wife's body. The strange look on his face jolted her out of her wretched self-pity.

Louisa wondered what he was thinking. It couldn't be easy for him. She put a hand on his arm.

"I'm sorry it had to be like this, Dickie."

With a deep sigh, he said, "You were right all along about her. I was completely taken in."

"I'm sorry...really I am. I know you loved her."

He laughed bitterly. "This damned war." Then added wistfully, "It's true, I did care for her once."

She allowed him a moment before saying, "You and she exchanged papers at the station?"

Dickie glanced at her, his face flushed red. "We used that method to pass on messages hidden in the text."

Louisa frowned. "So she was printing messages for the Germans? I suspected as much! Did you know?"

"That she was a double agent?" Dickie shook his head. "Not at first."

Louisa glared at the prone figure on the ground. Monique's association with Dickie had put them all into danger. And yet it was hard to blame him. The woman was an expert in deception.

"I swear I didn't know until that meeting in the café," he said, mopping perspiration off his brow. He glanced at Louisa. "It was when she called you Lulu. I had never divulged your codename to her."

Louisa recalled the words in his note. *Monique was about to expose you... Claude...*

At once, the penny dropped in Louisa's mind. "She got it from Claude!"

With a rueful smile, Dickie said, "I should have kicked the beggar out." He turned to Joe. "Come on, old chap, you look done in. We'd better go."

Ace drove them to an isolated farmhouse, far away from the village. As Dickie and Ace got out of the car, Louisa lifted her head and dried her swollen eyes. She shuddered. Even now she could hear the mob's taunts, see their crazed expressions, feel their sharp pokes and jabs. Wincing, she shuffled to the edge of the seat; every inch of her bruised body ached.

"Thank God you're safe," Joe said.

His eyes locked onto hers for a long moment. Touching her forehead gently with his, they sat in silence.

When he broke the contact to peel off the nun's habit disguising his shirt and trousers, she was bereft. She yearned to stay connected, to feel his life beat, to keep him with her. Her arms stole around his waist to pull him closer and she hid her face against his neck. She breathed in the scent of him and sighed deeply; she was home.

Joe's chin nuzzled her hair. His voice choked with barely controlled emotion as he mumbled, "Lovely, you do get yourself into some scrapes without me."

She smiled to herself and burrowed further into the hollow of his neck.

"You're shivering, old girl." He opened the car door. "We'd better go to the house."

Once settled into the warmth of the kitchen, Joe stroked her arm. His eyes twinkled wickedly as he murmured, "I once thought that girls were the weaker sex but you, my dear, have certainly opened my eyes."

"Mother always said I was a tomboy." She smiled.

He dropped a kiss onto her nose. "Your mum was right."

She gave him a teasing push and said modestly, "But you're the courageous hero. You helped me. I couldn't have done it without you." She angled her head to one side in thoughtful regard. Something still bothered her. "Earlier, on the roof..."

Joe pulled a face. "You've now discovered my deepest, darkest secret. But I'd thought I was over it." He frowned. "Must have been the stress of the plane crash, I reckon. My Spitfire nosedived at teeth-juddering speed."

"Frightening."

He shrugged. "Thank God I didn't have to bail out—now that *would* be scary."

A smile of agreement lit Louisa's face at his reference to her own dramatic entry into France. She said, "I was scared of the dark as a child. Is that when your fear began, too?"

"Yeah." Joe grinned. "I was a bit of a daredevil lad." And then he admitted, "You're not the only one who's taken some risks." He puffed out his cheeks and shook his head.

"I'd like to hear about them."

"I'll tell you sometime."

Louisa's heart jumped with hope. He was hinting at their future, one in which they would spend time together. She laughed, teasing, "Are there any more secrets or will I be forced to interrogate you?"

He grinned. "No need for that." His face grew serious as he put a finger under her chin, gently tilting her face up to his. "I'm more than willing to confess that I'm in love with you."

Her pulse began to race. "You said that it was the most passionate—"

"—night I'd ever had." His smile became rueful. "And you told me to—"

"Hush." Remembering, she grimaced as she put a finger to his lips. "I'm sorry that I doubted our future. But—"

"Now that the war's as good as ended—"

"Don't you dare," she continued with a happy smile, "leave this country without me!"

"I was hoping you'd say that." Joe captured her finger playfully between his teeth.

She held his gaze. "I love you, Joe Fisher."

Joe's smile lit up his face. His eyes searched hers for a long moment. "Marry me?"

"Yes," she whispered on a breath of pure joy. "Yes."

His eyelids lowered and their lips met.

And as excitement teased, a calm sense of peace settled in her heart. The future was there for them to do with as they wished.

Love was, after all, worth the risk.

About the Author

When I was fifteen, one of my favorite series of comic books was about the brave men and women of the French Resistance in World War Two. And it was the heroic female leader of these partisans who inspired the idea for my first published novel.

I live with my husband in the coastal city of Nelson, New Zealand.

Visit Cherie at www.cherieleclare.com

Thank you for purchasing this Wild Rose Press publication. For other wonderful stories of romance, please visit our on-line bookstore at www.thewildrosepress.com.

For questions or more information contact us at info@thewildrosepress.com.

The Wild Rose Press
www.TheWildRosePress.com

Lightning Source UK Ltd.
Milton Keynes UK
23 March 2010
151729UK00001B/49/P